MW01129035

The Unknown Disciple

Michael L. King

While based on actual events recorded in the King James Version of the New Testament, this is a work of fiction. Some of the characters, incidents, and dialogue are the products of the author's imagination. Much of the story is drawn from actual characters mentioned in the New Testament, with actual quotations from the New Testament being properly cited in the endnotes.

Cover artist: Sky Dodds

Scripture taken from the King James Version of the Bible.

WestBow Press books may be ordered through booksellers or by contacting:

WestBow Press
A Division of Thomas Nelson & Zondervan
1663 Liberty Drive
Bloomington, IN 47403
www.westbowpress.com
1 (866) 928-1240

ISBN: 978-1-9736-0171-5 (sc)
ISBN: 978-1-9736-0172-2 (hc)
ISBN: 978-1-9736-0170-8 (e)

Library of Congress Control Number: 2017913498

Print information available on the last page.

WestBow Press rev. date: 08/30/2017

To all the unknown disciples, especially my wife and my father, who live to love, bless, and serve others as Jesus himself would do, without the need for fame or recognition.

Contents

Preface

This book is a historical fiction based on events from the life of Jesus Christ as recorded in the four gospels, the greatest influence coming from the account of Luke. As an active witness of Jesus Christ, I have spent many years reading, pondering, and striving to understand and teach the New Testament. I have often marveled at the number of people whose stories have taught us major lessons, yet they themselves have remained unnamed and virtually unknown. These wonderings inspired me to reflect on their stories and try to see the events from their perspectives. These reflections led to dreams of the night that seemed so real that I awoke to record them, eventually resulting in the manuscript of The Unknown Disciple.

This book is intended for youth and adults of all faiths, but Christians will relate specifically to thoughts and ideas that have been taken from the pages of the New Testament as well as from thoughts and ideas shared by prominent Christian speakers and writers. While not quoted directly, these thoughts and ideas strongly influence the lessons that are derived from the experiences of the main character, the unknown disciple.

The fundamental teaching of this book is that to be a true follower and disciple of Jesus Christ does not require a position, a name, or a calling. As people seek to follow Jesus Christ and live his teachings, their lives are blessed, and they are able to learn lessons that even leaders, teachers, pastors, and clerics must learn.

A person becomes godly and Christlike by living Christ's teachings regardless of calling or recognition.

The approach taken in this work makes it different from many other Christian books. Because so many of us are unknown disciples, we find ourselves relating to the characters in the book, asking the same questions, feeling the same emotions, and seeking to understand ourselves as we learn from the lives of those who were with Jesus. By quoting exact passages from the New Testament and following the actual events recorded in the scriptures, people gain a sense of realism that allows the readers to discover gospel principles and truths from the New Testament that may have eluded them in their own readings. This book is not designed to be a doctrinal commentary of the New Testament but rather a "life lesson" perspective of the events that occurred for those in the time that Jesus walked among mankind. Exact scriptural passages are cited in the endnotes so that the reader can follow the story from the pages of the New Testament. This approach also lends validity to the idea that each gospel writer saw and recorded events according to their own unique perspectives.

Chapter 1

A Babe and a Beginning

Mine actually began as a pretty unremarkable story. Born to humble parents in the small, little-known town of Bethlehem, I grew up on the plains of Samaria. My parents were good people who worked hard; my father in the fields as a shepherd and my mother at home, feeding, clothing, and caring for her five small children, including me. I was the oldest, and therefore, I followed my father into the fields at a very young age. I was no more than five or six when Father first took me with him to tend to our small flock. I was taught how to tend and care for the sheep, learning how valuable they were in order to provide for our family. The wool they provided not only gave my mother wherewith to spin to make clothes for us but also provided enough that we were able to sell the best wool in the markets and earn a modest living.

I loved being with my father. He was a kind man, and though of meager means, he loved our family and worked hard to provide what he could with the little that he made from the sheep. While with him in the fields, I saw how tenderly and lovingly he cared for the flock. He had a name for each of the sheep and treated them as his children. I grew to love the sheep and enjoyed walking them to the pastures each morning where we would spend the day playing in the tall grasses that abounded along the hillsides. The sheep could eat their fill to grow more wool. My father would tell me stories of his youth and teach me how to care for and love the sheep.

As I grew older, Father moved us back to the small town of Bethlehem, where he was able to earn extra money tending to the large flocks of sheep that people used for the sacrifices at the nearby temple in Jerusalem. Though he was a simple hireling like the other men who tended to these flocks, my father acted more like a shepherd in caring for the sheep. He loved the flocks as his own, even though these sheep were not his property and would be sacrificed at the altars of the temple. My father told me that it was a great honor to tend to such sheep, whose sole purpose was to be sacrificed as a symbol of the Messiah, who would come to give his life for all the children of God.

I loved to hear my father speak of the Messiah. His coming had been long foretold, but no one—not even the rabbis and the priests—knew the time of his coming. Father spoke with such conviction and faith that I felt a special spirit each time he would talk of the Messiah. Though a poor and simple man who could not read, my father seemed to have a knowledge and faith about the Messiah that even the scribes did not possess. Many believed that the Messiah would be a great king who would lead the Jewish people to freedom and victory over the Romans who had occupied our lands from before my birth, but my father believed that the Messiah would be a humble shepherd who would love and care for the people and that he would live among them and tend to their needs just as Father cared for his sheep.

My father was often mocked by others, not just for what they called his naive and unlearned ideas but also because Father and his family were Samaritans. I discovered when we moved to Bethlehem that Samaritans were not liked by the Jews, and in fact, they were hated and rejected by many. My mother was from the tribe of Benjamin, but she had fallen in love with my father while on a journey to Galilee from her hometown of Bethlehem. Father had been serving at one of the roadside inns that bordered the land of Samaria and had cared for their animals when her family had stopped for the night. Mother said that she had noticed my father because of the kind and gentle way that he treated the animals. He treated them with a tenderness that touched my mother deeply. She believed that this man would also be kind and gentle to the children she desired to raise.

Father had noticed my mother as well and could not help but be captured by her humble grace and tender spirit. He noticed her watching him care for the animals and asked if she liked animals. She replied that she had always felt that the animals were more loyal and loving than many people. Father replied that he found animals to be more understanding of his thoughts and ideas than many people, and they usually let him get the last word. My mother giggled at his comment, and a friendship was born.

Mother was only sixteen at the time, but she was old enough that she could be considered for marriage. The man who sought her hand in marriage was much older, and he had made arrangements with my mother's father at one of the great feasts while on business in Jerusalem. Though she did not know the man, my mother was willing to do her duty to marry. Their family traveled to Galilee in order for my mother to formally meet this man and to make arrangements for the wedding, which was to occur in the next year. After meeting my father, however, my mother felt certain that he was the man she was to marry. She spoke with her mother and father about what she felt. Her father was upset and forbid her to think such thoughts, but her mother could see in her eyes that she was truly touched by this humble and loving man.

When their family departed in the morning, my mother was sad and quiet during the entire trip to Galilee. Her mother was kind and understanding and spoke lovingly to her during the journey, trying to console and prepare her for the events to come. When they arrived at Galilee, her father introduced my mother to the man she was to marry. The man was less than kind and inspected my mother as if she was a piece of merchandise he was about to purchase. He spoke harshly about my mother's lack of form and beauty and insisted upon a large dowry from the family if he were to take my mother to be his wife.

My mother's father became incensed at the man's churlish behavior and determined that this arrangement would not be best for his daughter or his family. They returned to Bethlehem, stopping again at the inn where my father worked. Seeing the joy of his daughter and gently persuaded by his wife, my later-to-become grandfather spoke to my father, even though he was a Samaritan. He saw that my father was a kind and loving soul who would treat his daughter with respect and gentleness, and so he agreed to allow him to visit and court his daughter. It was not long before arrangements were made for their wedding, even though it cost my mother's family their reputation and standing among the Jews in Bethlehem.

In coming to know my mother's parents, I have come to appreciate their willingness to seek the happiness of their daughter over the traditions and prejudices of their people. We were always welcome to their home in Bethlehem, and eventually, we moved there for my mother to be closer to her family. I guess you could say that I was taught from the beginning that the most important thing in life is family. Though we were half Samaritan, my brothers and sisters and I were as loved by our grandparents as any of their other grandchildren.

According to the Jewish oral law, because our mother was Jewish, we were considered Jewish. That did not seem to matter to many of the other relatives, who treated us with disdain. We were taught by our parents, however, not to revile back but to be kind to others regardless of their race, religion, or circumstance. Even when we were treated unfairly, we were taught to see each person as valuable in the sight of God, who was the Father of all.

It was this love of God and his understanding that all people are of great worth that moved my father to be kind and respectful to everyone. People could not help but accept and respect my father for his goodness and kindness to all. To be allowed to tend to the flocks for the sacrifice, though he was a Samaritan, was indeed rare, but Father's knowledge and care for the sheep had convinced the owners of the large flocks to bring him into their employ. Our family still maintained our own small flock, but the care and tending to them became primarily my responsibility, though I was only twelve years old.

One early spring evening while I was tending to my small flock outside of Bethlehem, my life and my unremarkable story began to change. I remember that the night was cool and clear, and every star in the sky seemed to be twinkling with a cheerful luster. The tiny town was crowded with many people who had come for the census and taxing, which had been commanded by the Roman leader, Caesar Augustus. Father and I were with a few other shepherds on a hillside outside of Bethlehem. We were tending to our flocks when a bright light began to gradually appear. The light grew brighter and brighter until it completely enveloped us all. Suddenly, within the light there stood a personage of the brightest white that I had ever seen. The other shepherds and I began to cower in fear, but my father stepped forward and gazed into the eyes of the man who stood before us.

The man informed us that he was an angel sent from God. Then he spoke words of joy and peace that were etched forever in my young and tender mind and that also stilled my fearful heart. "Fear not: for, behold I bring you good tidings of great joy, which shall be to all people. For unto you is born this day in the city of David, a Savior, who is Christ the Lord. And this shall be a sign unto you; ye shall find the babe wrapped in swaddling clothes, lying in a manger."[1]

Suddenly, there appeared in the skies a multitude of angels who were praising God and singing, "Glory to God in the highest, and on earth, peace to men of good will."[2]

The glorious strains of the angelic choir penetrated every fiber of my heart. I felt so full inside that I ached to sing with them, but I kept silent. My father wept openly at the joy we all felt. Then as suddenly as they appeared, the light gathered around them, and they disappeared into the night sky, leaving only the stars shining brightly above us. One star in particular seemed to shine brighter than all the rest as if marking the place of this magnificent event for all to see. Father turned and spoke to us all, "Let us now go even unto Bethlehem, and see this thing which is come to pass, which the Lord hath made known unto us."[3]

Leaving our flocks to the care and keeping of the Lord, we went with great haste to Bethlehem to see this wondrous sight. We knew the town's bedding stables and inns, so we followed the feelings in our hearts in search of the place foretold by the angel. Not far from one of the inns, we came to a humble cave, from which emanated a holy light. As we entered, we found a beautiful maiden held closely in the arms of her husband; and in a small manger next to her was an infant boy wrapped and sleeping gently in the hay. A holy and sacred light shone from his countenance. We could not help but lowly sing anthems of praise and adoration. "Oh, holy night, Son of God, love's pure light!" We echoed the message of the angels, "Hallelujah! Hallelujah! Jesus Christ is born. This, this is Christ the King!"[4]

I felt as if my heart would burst from the sheer joy that I felt in the presence of this pure, holy, and innocent child. I caught the mother's gaze and asked if she would permit me to kiss her child. She smiled brightly, placed her hand upon my cheek, nodded her approval, and said gently, "His name is Jesus." I bowed low over the manger, placed my lips gently upon his forehead, and whispered, "Jesus." I felt a power and light that filled my soul with a desire to be good, wholesome, and true to everything that was good and right. I raised my head and returned that sweet mother's smile with one of my own, which would not leave my face for several days. The incredible joy that I felt finally burst forth from my eyes in the form of tears that ran like rivers down my cheeks. I laughed softly and turned to look upon my father, who had moved over by the father of the infant boy. I could tell that they were kindred spirits—good men of the earth who lived by a standard of honesty, integrity, goodness, purity, and virtue. The babe's father reached out and placed his large and rugged hand upon my shoulder. As he looked into my eyes, I could see why he was chosen to be the example of manhood and fatherhood to this holy child, whom the angel had declared to us was the Savior, our awaited and beloved Messiah.

As we left the humble cave, I felt as if I had walked upon the most sacred ground on earth. I marveled that the chosen Messiah had come in such humble circumstances, but it was as my father had said it would be. I asked my father how he knew that this was how the Messiah would come. He gently placed his arm around my shoulders and said, "Because I have known the love of God for me since I was a young boy. I have known that God would show that love by sending his Son among those of us who are in the most desperate need of hope. Never forget the joy and peace that you felt tonight, Son. I am certain that you will have a chance to meet this Messiah again, and you will witness the miracle of his love in your life."

Chapter 2

The Loss, the Forgetting, and the Forgiving

Father's words proved to be prophetic. I did not hear much of Jesus or his parents for many years. I heard stories that they had fled to Egypt to avoid an unthinkable edict given by King Herod. In jealousy and fear of the child who might replace him as king, Herod had commanded that all children under the age of two were to be killed. Some of my young cousins were taken during that heart-wrenching experience. The land was filled with continual mourning and weeping for the lost children of innocence. I was concerned that the holy child might have been taken before he even had a chance to become our Messiah, but my father assured me that God would protect his Son and make sure that Joseph was guided in what he must do to keep the child safe.

Several years passed, and I heard nothing about Jesus. I had not married, but I worked hard to earn as much money as I could by tending sheep. With the help of my father, I was hired to tend one of the large flocks of the sacrificial sheep in a pasture near the city of Jerusalem. With so many sacrifices required by Jewish law, there was always a great need for sheep to be offered. I earned sufficient funds to allow me to move from the home of my parents and begin to seek to increase my wealth, station, and standing in society.

Not many months after leaving the home of my parents, tragedy struck my family. Both my parents and all my brothers and sisters became violently ill. Healers were called, and I came to try to give aid; however, I was not allowed into our home for fear that I, too, would become ill. I prayed to God for his help, but no answer came. My mother was the first to succumb to the sickness followed by my youngest brother. Eventually, all my brothers and sisters were taken, leaving my father mourning the loss of his family while on the verge of death himself. My anguish became more than I could bear as I watched my father—the best man I had ever known—slip from this life to the next. My grief overwhelmed me. I felt abandoned and lost. Why had God taken my family? Why did God not heal them?

I felt distanced from God. I could not feel his spirit or hear his voice. I ceased to pray and turned myself completely to seeking the things of the world. I threw myself into my work to keep myself occupied. I sought any way to earn more money and to increase my wealth. I continued to tend sheep, but I sought for the chance to purchase a flock of my own and establish wealth and position in society.

Twelve years had passed since I had witnessed the angelic announcement of the babe in Bethlehem. It all seemed as nothing more than a distant memory. The feeling I had felt when kissing the baby had long since been replaced by bitterness and anger toward God for the loss of my family. I continued to busy myself with my work, taking extra jobs to take sheep to Jerusalem for special events. Passover was a particularly busy time for me. Many people from all over the Holy Land would travel to Jerusalem for the celebration. Passover required that each family offer a lamb as a part of the feast. The lambs had to be male, firstborn, and without blemish in order to meet the specifications of the law. The lamb was to be a reminder of the lambs that had been sacrificed in the days of Moses so that the angel of death would pass over the houses of the Israelites, who had placed the blood of the lamb on their doorposts. This was also to symbolize the coming Messiah who would save Israel from death.

I spent most of my time during the week of the Passover selling my master's lambs that would meet the required specifications. As most of the people would come to worship at the temple during this festival week, I built a pen for the lambs as near to the temple as I was allowed. I also set up a small tent alongside the pen in which to rest at night. It was a very busy time in the city, and many vendors filled the main square to sell their wares. I busied myself with doing all I could to provide lambs for the people. My master had promised me extra wages if I could sell all the lambs that he had sent. As every family needed lambs for the Passover, I was determined to sell all the lambs of my master's flock and earn the extra money promised.

The evening of the Passover drew near, and I found myself still in the city, trying to sell the last lamb of my flock. A man and his young son came by my tent, seeking a lamb for their family. They had traveled to the city from Nazareth. As I sold the father the lamb, the boy asked me where I was planning to celebrate Passover. I had no plans to celebrate the Passover. I had no desire to think of God and his promised deliverance. God had not delivered me or my family, so what did I have to celebrate?

As I stammered for an answer, the boy looked penetratingly into my eyes and said, "Father, could he join us for the feast?" A bit surprised, I politely declined. The father said that they would be honored to have me join them, but I refused. I told them that I had plans to spend the feast with my family. As I told this blatant lie, I saw hurt and pain in the eyes of the boy. It was as if he knew that I was not telling the truth. He tried again to invite me to join them, but my stubborn pride caused me to resist his kind offer. I was afraid that by accepting his invitation, they would detect that I held no respect for Passover. The only care that filled my heart was the accumulation of wealth and importance in society.

The boy could see that I was not going to change my mind, so he and his father turned to leave. As they departed, the boy looked back at me and caught my eye. I saw a love, purity, and goodness that took my breath away. I felt something that I had not felt in nearly twelve years. I ached to ask the boy's name, but my pride prevented me. I was ashamed that I had not recognized him when he had approached my tent. He did not have an outward appearance or carriage of a Messiah. He was a normal boy of no outstanding features, but deep inside I knew that it was him; however, in my shame, I could not bring myself to call them back, admit my deceit, and go with them. Remorse, guilt, and regret began to fill my heart. I feared that I had missed the chance to be the good person that I had desired to be in my heart as I had kissed the sweet, tender babe so many years before.

An emptiness overcame me as I watched them disappear into the city. I made my way to a nearby market, purchased some cheese to supplement the bread I had brought for my evening meal, and then retired for the evening. Sleep fled from me as I tossed and turned, reflecting the turmoil in my heart and mind. I remembered the light of purity and goodness in the eyes of the boy. I was certain that this was the Messiah I had seen in the manger. I wondered if I would ever see him again. I was determined that if given the chance, I would admit my mistake and seek his forgiveness. With this thought in my heart, I did something that I had seldom done since the passing of my father and dear mother. I prayed. I struggled to find the words. After several attempts, I simply began to weep. The thought of the babe in the manger came vividly to my mind. It was as if I was there again, bowing gently to kiss his brow. Gradually, I began to feel peace. Thoughts of my experience in Bethlehem filled my mind, and a feeling of love entered my heart as I drifted off to sleep.

The next morning was brisk and chill, and I didn't want to get out from under the soft woolen blanket that covered me. I could hear movement outside of my tent, and I knew that people were beginning to pack their wares to return to their homes. I reluctantly pulled myself from under the blanket and sat up. I contemplated my return to my master's home to report that I had sold all the sheep. I began to think about the things I could purchase with the extra money I would receive. Invigorated by the thought that I would soon have extra money, I quickly packed up my few belongings and made my way to the outskirts of Jerusalem.

The thought of the extra money helped me to forget the pain and guilt of the previous evening, and I began to rationalize that it probably wasn't the Messiah after all. Deep inside, however, there was a nagging feeling in my heart that I had missed my chance to acknowledge him and spend a blessed Passover with him and his family.

Upon my return to the home of my master, I showed him the money that I had gained for him in selling all the lambs. He anxiously took the coins, smiled broadly, and turned to walk away. Then almost as an afterthought, he returned to pay me my wages, but without the bonus that I had expected. I realized that his thoughts were only on the money just as mine had been the night before when I had refused my own Passover worship. Disappointed, I turned to leave. Suddenly, he called me back and said, "I believe that I forgot the bonus I promised you." Grateful, I turned to receive the extra money. As he handed me the few extra coins, he said, "My friends at the feast told me that you had been so diligent in selling the lambs that you continued to sell into the evening of the feast." I nodded. He asked me if I would like to make even more money by taking a group of sheep back to Jerusalem.

I eagerly accepted his proposal and asked, "When would you like me to return?"

"Immediately," he replied. "It appears that with so many of the lambs being sacrificed for the feast, there is an urgent need for animals for the daily sacrifices. If you will return now with the sheep, I will give you an additional bonus. Sell all these sheep, and I will give you a small flock of your own."

Excited by this opportunity to have my own flock, I quickly gathered my belongings and made my way back to Jerusalem. It was approaching evening as I arrived at the spot where I had been for the Passover. I set up my tent and quickly made my way to the temple to contact the priests and let them know that I had sheep for their morning sacrifices. Being a Samaritan, I was not allowed into the temple itself, so I went to the outer wall and asked to speak to one of the priests. It took several moments before one of the priests came out to talk to me. I told him about the sheep, but he seemed agitated and distracted. He assured me that he would inform the others, but he needed to return into the temple. Apparently, a young boy was in the temple teaching things that caused all the priests and scribes to marvel and ponder, and he did not want to miss what was being said.

As the priest hurried back inside of the temple, a stunned feeling came over me. Surely, this had to be Jesus, but why would he be teaching in the temple at such a young age? Had he declared himself to be the Messiah? Was he beginning his ministry? My mind became a swirl of confused thoughts and questions. I moved closer to the entryway to the temple to see if I could catch a glimpse of Jesus. One of the Levites stepped into my path and asked that I step back from the gate, allowing room for those who were allowed to enter. I moved away and found a spot where I could sit and watch the gate. If this was Jesus, I was determined that I would not miss the opportunity to meet and speak with him.

The sun had set, and darkness began to envelope the square. Torches were lit along the streets to light the way for those still traveling to their homes. I heard noises and saw a group of men coming out of the temple with a young boy in their midst. I could see that it was indeed the boy who had approached me with his father the night before. I moved forward toward the group. The priest to whom I had spoken earlier saw me and said, "I told you that we would talk in the morning regarding the sheep."

I did not look his direction, but I focused my attention on the lad. He gazed into my eyes, and I felt again the desire to be good and virtuous in everything that I pursued, just as I had felt at the manger. I was surprised that Jesus's father and mother were not with him. I asked him about them, and he assured me that they were fine and were on their way back to Nazareth. "But why aren't you with them?" I inquired. He told me that he had work to do for his Father here in the city. A bit confused, the priests asked the boy where he intended to spend the night. He pointed at me and said, "My friend will provide me a place to sleep." A bit startled, I assured the priests that I would care for the boy, though deep in my heart, I knew that it was he who would care for me.

Satisfied, the priests departed, and I stood alone in the street, gazing into those eyes, which seemed to penetrate every fiber of my soul. I stammered, not knowing what to say. I began slowly to apologize for the lie I had told the previous night, but he stopped me short, grasped my hand, looked into my eyes, and said, "Worry not, my friend. I know thy heart and see thy desire to be good. The end of your path is still unwritten, but you have made the first steps in making right that which you have done wrong. Thank you for waiting upon me while I was about my Father's business. Thank you for agreeing to take me into your home for the night."

I humbly informed him that I had nothing but a small tent and woolen blanket to offer. He assured me that he had slept in much less with only a bed of straw and swaddling clothes to keep him from the elements. I looked upon him and saw in his countenance the light of the babe in Bethlehem and knew that he knew that I had come to him as a young shepherd boy. Tears began to well up in my eyes. I reached out and placed my hand about his face and then pulled him to me. His embrace warmed my soul and caused the chill of the evening to disappear.

We walked back to my tent and I shared my meager meal with him. Before we partook, he took the small loaf of bread, broke it carefully, and then gave thanks to God for his bounteous blessings. Never had I heard anyone pray in such a manner. It was as if he was speaking directly to God. He did not recite the typical prayer that was offered at mealtime but genuinely expressed gratitude and love to God for what was provided. He then thanked God for hearts that were open to receive him and share with him what little they had. He pleaded that God would care for and provide for all who gave so willingly to others in need. As I heard this young boy pray to God on my behalf, my heart melted. I felt love and joy that I had only known on that holy night so long ago. When he finished praying, he handed me the loaf he had broken. As I partook of the crusty bread

I had carried for weeks, I was amazed at its delicious sweetness. Its taste was what I imagined manna tasted like in the days of Moses.

Though our meal was small, I felt filled and content. I asked him again about his parents, thinking that they might be worried that he had not accompanied them on the return trip to Nazareth. He assured me that they would be fine and would soon discover that he was not among them. He said that they would return two days hence. During that time, he told me that he had much to teach in the temple and would return there each day. He asked if he could return each night to sleep in my tent. I felt honored and humbled at his request and assured him that he would always be welcome in my tent. He then gazed upon me with a look that left me wondering what he knew about what was yet to come in my life.

As we concluded our meal, I realized now the opportunity I had missed in not joining Jesus and his family for the Passover feast. I could only imagine the feelings and blessings I had missed in not accepting his invitation to come. Though he was a boy, I felt as if I was the younger of the two of us and that I had much to learn about his mission. He thanked me for allowing him to come into my tent. "Jesus," I said, "it is I who should thank you that you have given me this opportunity after I had rejected your invitation into your home."

He smiled and assured me that God provides us many opportunities to receive his grace, even when we do not reach out to receive him. "There are times," he said, "when God aches to hold us and heal our heartaches. Many times, however, in the face of trials, many people do not look upward but cast their eyes downward in doubt and fail to find the strength to endure challenges that come as a part of life."

As I listened to the wisdom of this young boy, I realized his words reflected how I had responded to the loss of my family. Rather than seek strength from God to accept their passing back into his presence, I had become bitter that God had not spared their lives. I was more concerned about my aching heart than accepting the difficult challenges that life presents. I looked away from Jesus, but he gently placed his hand upon my cheek, turned my face to his, and assured me that God knew my pain and would heal my hurt. As I finally lay down to rest that night, my thoughts and dreams were of heaven and heavenly things. I do not recall ever having such a peaceful night's sleep.

The next couple of days, I busied myself in selling my master's sheep. As he had said, there was a great need for the sheep at this time, so I was able to sell all of them. Each night Jesus would come to my tent, we would share a meal, and he would teach me of the things of his Father. I marveled at his wisdom and understanding for a boy so young. He spoke with a quiet knowing, which touched me deeply. Each word he spoke resonated with a truth I had felt in my heart and seemed to know even as he spoke it.

I felt that I could never be the same person I had been prior to listening to Jesus, and I prayed each night that that feeling would never leave me. I felt as I had long ago in Bethlehem when I pleaded that I would always remember the feeling I had when I had kissed Jesus as a baby in the manger. I was determined that this experience would be different. I was older now and would surely not forget such a powerful experience eating, conversing, and sharing my tent with the Messiah.

The days passed quickly, and it was just as Jesus said it would be. His parents arrived in Jerusalem, worried and wondering what had become of their son. I was outside the temple when they arrived. The father recognized me from our brief encounter a few nights before and asked, "Sir, has thou seen our son? We have traveled three days in search of him. Knowest thou where he might be?" I responded that I had indeed seen their son and had housed him in my tent each night. I informed them that they would find Jesus inside the temple, teaching the priests. When they found him in the temple, they entreated him to come with them, and he agreed. As they were leaving the temple, I heard Mary ask him with the aching of a mother's heart, "Son, why hast thou thus dealt with us? Behold, thy father and I have sought thee sorrowing." With a tender yet knowing response, Jesus answered, "How is it that ye sought me? Wist ye not that I must be about my Father's business?"[5]

Having sat with Jesus for the past two nights, I knew that he was gently but firmly reminding Mary who his true Father was. Mary embraced her son, and Joseph encircled them both within his broad embrace. Though worried and concerned, neither Mary nor Joseph seemed upset at his reply, knowing that he truly had important work to do that had little to do with being a carpenter. As they passed by me, preparing to leave the city for their return trip to Nazareth, they thanked me for caring for their son. I assured them that I was the one who had been blessed by his presence and thanked them for their care of such a magnificent child. In their warmth and understanding, I felt again the wisdom of God in sending Jesus to such humble and wonderful parents.

I looked one more time into the eyes of Jesus and felt his great love and saw again the vision of who I was to become. I did not know at the time the road that I would have to travel in order to become the person he saw, but I felt a sense of hope at what lay ahead for me. I desired with all my soul to become what I saw in his eyes and to live what I felt in my heart as he taught me the words of life.

Chapter 3

Settling as a Samaritan

Determined to live according to the things that I had learned from Jesus, I tried my best to live honestly among my fellow man and share with them the joy I felt in knowing that the Messiah had come. I found myself mocked on every side by the Jews with whom I associated as I tried to tell them of my experiences. I remembered the way that they had mocked my father when he had spoken of his feelings about the Messiah. I soon began to see that as a people, the Jews were too proud and hard-hearted to accept any thoughts of a Messiah who did not come as a conqueror and king. Finding myself becoming embittered by their arrogance and disdain toward me, I sold the small flock I had been given by my master and used the money to begin a business of buying and selling various wares in the markets.

I soon realized, however, that most Jews were hesitant to buy from one whose blood was mixed with the Samaritans. Unable to establish my business to any degree in Jerusalem, I moved north to the city of Sychar in the land of the Samaritans. In ancient days Sychar had been a prominent city, holy to all the house of Israel. Formerly known as Shechem, it lay in a fertile valley between the mountains of Mt. Gerizim and Mt. Ebal. It was the site where Joshua put Israel under covenant to obey and follow God.

After Israel and Judah had divided into two separate kingdoms, many from the kingdom of Israel had intermarried with the Syrians who had invaded the land, thus leaving them unclean and impure in the eyes of those from the tribe of Judah. When the Jews refused to allow the Samaritans to help in the rebuilding of the temple in Jerusalem, the Samaritans actually worked to prevent the Jews from building the temple in the days of Nehemiah. The Samaritans became bitter enemies of the Jews and built a temple of their own close to the city of Shechem on Mt. Gerizim. Shechem became a cultural and social center for the Samaritans.

Sychar now stood in the place where Shechem had been and was the capital of Samaria. Though it was the center of Samaritan life, Sychar was also close to the place of Jacob's well, which held special significance to the Jews. While many Jews avoided traveling through Samaria because of their feelings toward Samaritans, the draw of a place as sacred and holy as Jacob's well allowed for them to make an exception to their oral laws regarding their dealings with Samaritans.

Thus situated, Sychar provided a perfect place for me to engage in buying, selling, and trading with both Samaritans and Jews. Employing the principles of love and kindness that I had learned from Jesus, my business began to thrive. While working in the markets, I met a young woman of striking features and brilliant countenance. She had been orphaned as a young child and was taken into the home of some wealthy landowners near Sychar. Treated more as a servant or possession than a daughter, she was constantly running errands for her masters. Despite her difficult lot in life, her pleasant smile and cheerful attitude told me that she was her own person and not enslaved by those who thought her to be their property.

After several encounters with her in the marketplace, I sought out her owners to request her hand in marriage. They agreed, but they required a hefty dowry from me, even though she was not truly their daughter. My success in the markets allowed me the means to meet their demands. To their surprise, I offered them double the dowry, as I wanted the entire world to know what I felt she was worth. It served to let her know that to me she was a woman of great worth—more than the world would ever see. We were wed and lived in my home near the markets.

My life seemed to have followed a course of joy and contentment in choosing to follow the things I had learned from Jesus. I thought about him often, wondering when he would begin his ministry among the people. While I anxiously awaited that day, I continued to keep myself busy in providing a comfortable living for my wife and our desired family. My business was flourishing, but we experienced repeated sorrows in our attempts to have children. We felt the heartbreak of miscarriage and lost two children at birth.

The years passed. I began to travel more frequently to Jerusalem to buy and sell merchandise for my business. On one occasion while traveling between Jerusalem and Jericho, I found a young man lying stripped and beaten alongside of the road. I quickly dismounted and gave what aid I could. Binding up his wounds, pouring in wine for cleansing and oil to help the healing, I placed him upon my horse and took him to a nearby inn. I tended to the man through the night, changing his wrappings and feeding him a bit of broth with a morsel of bread and cheese. By morning he was still unable to travel, so I left money for the innkeeper and asked him to tend to my friend until I returned from my business in Jerusalem, assuring him that I would make good for all services rendered.

To my great joy, when I returned a few days later, the man was much better and on his way to recovery. I stayed with him one more night. I learned that his name was Luke, a Gentile not of the Jewish nation who was traveling through Israel. He had fallen among thieves while making his journey from Jerusalem to Jericho. He said that others had passed by him and that none had stopped. He had given up hope and resigned himself to the fact that he would die on the wayside. He lost consciousness, and when he awoke he found himself here in the inn.

He thanked me repeatedly for rendering him aid. I told him that I was simply following the counsel of a young boy whom I had known years before. I hesitated to tell him that I knew him to be the

Messiah, but I felt a prompting that he would accept my teaching, so I told him of Jesus and my experiences in coming to know him as the Son of God. Luke listened with fascination and asked what had become of the boy. I told him that I did not know but that I was certain that he would soon be coming among the common people to help them and to heal them.

Luke told me that while he was recovering in the inn, he had felt the desire to become a physician in order to help others who may be sick or hurt. I told him that I felt that helping others was one of the greatest works in which we could engage ourselves in this life. As we parted company, he told me that when he returned to his homeland, he would always remember my kindness. I assured him that we would forever be friends and brothers in God. He again thanked me. We embraced, and I rode back to Sychar.

The weeks and months melted into years. My business continued to flourish, but my wife and I were still unable to have children. I began to wonder why the Lord was withholding this great blessing from me and my dear, sweet wife, who wanted nothing more than to be a mother. I was nearing my fortieth year, and I felt like we should stop trying to have children. But my wife insisted that we continue to make the attempt. She became pregnant later that year, but I did not hold any hope that we would indeed have a child as we had traveled this road many times.

As the time of my wife's delivery arrived, the midwife came from the room with a very sullen look. I was prepared for the news that we had lost another child, but she informed me of even more terrible news. Not only had the baby not survived, but my wife had given her life in trying to deliver the child. A shock ran through my heart that seemed to break it into several pieces. I burst into the room where my wife lay lifeless upon the bed. All of my tears, all of my kisses, and all of my pleadings to God did not revive her. I felt as if my own life had ended with hers.

My inconsolable sorrow was followed by a despair that emptied any happiness, joy, or hope from my heart. In anguish I called out to God, but I heard and received nothing. Night after endless night,

I poured out my heart in prayer, seeking some semblance of peace, some soul-reviving answer from above. The heavens were silent, and I felt abandoned by the very God I thought I had come to know through the boy Jesus. Memories of the loss of my family flooded back into my mind, consuming the hope that I had felt during my time with Jesus. Everything I had ever loved had been taken from me by the very God whom Jesus said was our Father.

Desperate for some sense of relief, I thought about my experiences with Jesus and tried to recall the feelings that had swelled within me while I had sat with him in my tent so many years before. As I thought on that experience, however, I began to wonder how the God that Jesus said loved us all could allow such a thing to happen. I felt bitterness begin to fill my heart. I fought to find the sweet feelings of hope and forgiveness that I had previously felt, but my grief would not allow any light to penetrate the darkness that was beginning to envelope my heart.

More determined, I pleaded for the Lord to send me some sort of light to help me see my way out of the darkness. But each time I would start to feel that he understood my sorrow, my doubting heart and mind would ask in anger, "If you understand, then why will you not remove this pain? Why did you let my family and the only woman I have ever loved die? Why did you not give us the blessing of children?"

Despite my efforts to resist, grief filled my mind with doubts, which caused me to lose the faith that I had sworn so determinedly to maintain. I began to respond to others with the same bitterness and resentment that I felt in my heart toward God. Soon my business began to suffer and eventually fell into ruin. In less than two years from the passing of my wife, I lost everything I had worked to attain. Embarrassed about what I had become, I refused the help of friends who tried to come to my aid and comfort me. I lived on the streets of Sychar, begging for food enough to keep me alive.

One day while I was sitting on a corner in the market square, several men came into the city to purchase food at the market. I begged one of them for just a morsel of bread or something to eat, but he told me that they were there to obtain food for their master. As he was about to turn away from me, another of the men said to the one who had refused me, "Brother, what do you think our master would have us do?" With a knowing look, he smiled and turned back to hand me a half of a loaf of bread. He invited me to come with them to meet his master, but I refused; choosing to wallow in my own self-pity and despair. The men bade me a blessing and left the city. Shortly after the men departed, a woman of the city whom I had seen many times in the market came and stood on a large stone in the center of the square. She spoke in a loud voice for all to hear, "Come, see a man which told me all things that ever I did: is not this the Christ?"[6]

Her words caught my attention, and I listened intently to her sayings. She was known in the city to have been married several times and was now living with a man who was not her husband. Some began to mock her and think her mad at such expressions. "The Christ?" they queried. "And why would the Christ come to you, one who is little more than a harlot?" She paid them no heed and insisted that she had met the man at Jacob's well, and though he was a Jew, he had asked her for water. He then promised her living water if she would but request it of him.

As she spoke, I felt hope spring up within me. Could this be Jesus, now of full age and teaching among the people? I went to the woman and asked if she knew the name of the man to whom she had spoken. She said that she did not know his name, but when she spoke to him of the Messiah who would come and who would be called Christ, he had responded, "I that speak unto thee am he."[7] She told me that as she spoke to him, she felt a love that she had never known, and now she wanted with all her heart to be a better person and to live everything that was good and right.

Her words pierced me to my center. I had felt those same things years before. I knew from her words that this was indeed Jesus, the Christ. I asked the woman where I might find him. She told me that he was still at the well, meeting with his disciples, who had come into town to buy provisions. They had just come from the Passover in Jerusalem and were on their way back to Nazareth in Galilee. Nazareth! This was the place to which Jesus and his family had returned when he was a boy. Surely, this had to be him! I ran out to the place of Jacob's well to see for myself. Several other men who had also wondered at the woman's words journeyed to the well to see for themselves.

As soon as I arrived at the well, I knew him. His eyes still radiated the light and love that I remembered when he shared my tent as a boy. When Jesus saw me, he came toward me and extended his arms to me. I fell into his embrace. And such an embrace! My heart melted as I remembered again all that I had felt before when I had been in his presence. I began to weep and seek his forgiveness. He grasped my hands as he had done before, looked into my eyes, and assured me that God had seen my sorrow and had heard my cries. It was as if he knew all that I had experienced and truly comprehended my pain and anguish. I sought for the words to say, but I could only manage sobs of release as I fell at his feet, bathing his feet with my tears. It was as if all of my sorrow, pain, grief, bitterness, and guilt were being laid at his feet. He knelt down in front of me, took my face in his hands, and kissed my forehead. "I have shared your tent, and now I have shared your sorrow. Will you now come and follow me? I cannot promise that the road will be easy, but I can promise that you will find the peace and comfort that you have been seeking."

As Jesus spoke of the road ahead, I again wondered about what he knew about my life and my journey. Each time I had been with Jesus, he had lifted my vision and restored my hope in what I might become. I determined to follow him regardless of where that road might lead me. I was certain that I had found what I had been seeking ever since the day that I kissed Jesus as an infant—to do good and be good in my daily dealings with others. Slowly, I arose to my feet, nodded my head, and told him that I would follow him wherever the road might lead. I had no idea how much I still had to learn and do before I could become the man Jesus saw in me, but I took the first steps on that journey in choosing to follow Jesus.

Jesus invited me to come and allow him to immerse me into the waters of a nearby stream as a symbol of my entrance into the kingdom of God. At first, I did not understand the need for me to be "baptized" as he called it, but he explained that this immersion was to symbolize my complete commitment to following his teachings and my determination to obey God. He also helped me to see that this was to symbolize the death of my old self, and my birth into a new way of living. "This re-birth," he said, "will signify your beginning of a new life in God."

I willingly agreed and followed Jesus into the stream. After praying to the Father, he lowered me into the waters. As I came forth from the water, I felt new. I felt like I had been given a chance to start my life again, this time more committed and focused on following the commandments of God. I did not realize at the time, but this was just the first of many steps that I would need to take in order to become the man that God wanted me to be.

Chapter 4

Struggling through Stormy Seas

Word began to spread throughout all the regions of Israel regarding the ministry and miracles of Jesus. Throngs of people would gather to him as he preached in the countryside of Galilee. Though the multitudes were great, I felt that Jesus knew and loved each one of us. His love seemed infinite in its reach but intimate in its impact. There were times when I had the chance to talk privately with him. We talked of the challenges that life continually presented, even when we choose to do what is right. "Sometimes the right choices lead us down the most difficult paths," he said with conviction in his voice. He then assured me that while life's journey might bring sorrow, pain, and loss, it would also bring to us the qualities of patience, perseverance, hope, and charity toward others if we would but turn to God in submissive humility and faith. Here he paused and looked out over a group that was beginning to gather about us. I could see the love in his eyes for the people. Then he looked directly at me and said, "Only as we see and love others as God loves them and lose thought of ourselves in serving them can we gain the attributes necessary to develop a godly character and do for others what must be done regardless of the price or sacrifice."

I wondered at Jesus's words to see others as God sees them. What did he mean to lose myself in serving others? As we walked near the Sea of Gennesaret, I sought another occasion to speak with him privately. Jesus became quiet and somber as I inquired about losing myself. He then looked penetratingly into my eyes and said, "When we think of ourselves, we begin to wonder why things do not go as we desire when we experience some of the bitterness that comes from this mortal experience. We then feel lost and forsaken. This can cause us to question God and his love for us. It is then that we must not choose to become bitter but to trust that in God's time and in his way, he will lead us to the light. One of the greatest challenges of life," he confided, "is to not allow the bitter experiences of life to cause us to become bitter."

His words cut deep into my heart. He somehow knew the bitterness that I had allowed to overtake me and to lead me down roads of despair and self-destruction. My eyes broke his penetrating gaze, and I looked ashamedly to the ground. Gently, he lifted my chin to gaze once again into his eyes, and I could see his love, his comprehension, and his forgiveness. I felt a sense of reconciliation. The bitterness was now gone. Hope was restored, and I could move forward with renewed faith in God.

I felt changed and made new. I wanted again to do and be the good that I saw in him. I marveled at the power Jesus possessed to not only teach these elevating and divine truths but to live them fully day to day in his life as well. His life reflected his teaching. I longed to possess that power within me, but I found myself continually returning to old thoughts and feelings despite my desire to be otherwise.

I wondered how it was possible for me to hold on to the good feelings I had repeatedly experienced and act continually in accordance with God's will. Jesus assured me that reconciling one's self to God's will constituted one of the greatest efforts of life. "There are times," he said, "when God will ask of us to drink of a cup most bitter that his will may be done to bring about the salvation and exaltation of our brothers and sisters." Then with a knowledge I did not understand at the time, he said, "I came down from heaven, not to do mine own will, but the will of him that sent me.[8] Any man, who desires to come after me, must be willing to deny himself, take up his cross, and follow me."[9]

As he finished speaking with me, Jesus noticed that a multitude had gathered around us. Desiring to address the whole group but knowing how difficult it would be for all to see and hear him, he entered into one of two empty ships along the shore of the Sea of Gennesaret where we had been talking. He requested that the owner thrust out a little from the land so that he might be heard by the people. The owner humbly complied without complaint or question. Jesus then sat down in the boat and taught us as we sat along the shore.

The gentle ebb and flow of the lake seemed to bring his words continually to the shore and into my heart. I felt as if the very water and elements responded to his voice, serving a master they recognized from their creation. His was the voice of more than a carpenter but of a God, who had come down among us to not only teach us but to show us how to live in harmony with God, with nature, and with one another. I felt the joy and peace I had felt before as I had kissed Jesus as a babe in the manger. Oh, that I could hold on to such moments and live the words that I heard him speak. I longed for a lasting and permanent change.

As Jesus concluded, he said unto Simon, the owner of the boat, "Launch out into the deep, and let down your nets for a haul." Simon responded, "Master, we have toiled all the night and have taken nothing: nevertheless, at thy word I will let down the net."[10] I was impressed at his faith to do as Jesus had asked of him.

As they cast out into the lake, I dangled my feet in the rippling lake and pondered on the words Jesus had spoken. Such words of truth brought light and understanding that surpassed anything that I had previously understood concerning God and my relationship to him. Quietly, I prayed his forgiveness for my lack of faith in him during the time of my wife's passing. Her death no longer troubled me, and I somehow knew that all would be well with us in a time yet to come. I felt that I would see her again and that once more we would embrace. I also felt certain that one day we would have the children we had deeply desired.

My thoughts were interrupted by shouts from out on the ship. Simon and the men on his boat were shouting to their partners to bring the other boat to help them bring in the great haul of fish they had captured in their nets. I watched as they brought fish after fish aboard their vessels, causing both ships to drop lower and lower into the water. I thought that the ships would sink with the multitude of fish they had brought onboard. I saw Simon fall before Jesus, and I had a sense of what he was feeling. I could not hear everything that was said, but I knew that Simon's life would not be the same from this point forward.

When they were finally able to get the ships to shore, Simon Peter, his brother Andrew, and his partners, James and John, all left their nets to follow Jesus. I could only imagine, but it seemed that the number of fish they had brought must have been sufficient to supply their families for quite some time. Leaving all behind, they began to follow in the steps of Jesus just as numerous others had done, including me.

Not all who came to hear Jesus, however, felt his great power and wisdom. They seemed to challenge him on every point of doctrine that he taught. The Pharisees, Sadducees, and the Scribes—those learned in the law and traditions of the fathers—were particularly critical of Jesus.

I remember one occasion when a man was brought who had palsy, a disease that left him unable to move or to care for himself. Some of his friends carried the man to the roof of the house where Jesus was teaching, removed some of the tiling, and lowered their friend through the roof. I smiled at their determination and wit in order to help their friend. Seeing their faith, Jesus was impressed at their efforts and said to the man, "Man, thy sins be forgiven thee."[11]

At first, I thought that I had heard him incorrectly, but I heard some of the Scribes around me murmur that he had spoken blasphemy, asking, "Who can forgive sins, but God alone?"[12] They spoke in low, muttered tones from the back of the house where I was standing, but it was as if Jesus knew their thoughts. He moved toward them and asked, "What reason ye in your hearts?" They did not answer, remaining smug and aloof, and they looked indignantly upon Jesus. Jesus continued, "Does it require more power to forgive sins than to make the sick rise up and walk?" Still, there was no reply from his accusers. He then stated, "But that ye may know that the Son of Man hath power upon earth to forgive sins," he said unto the sick of the palsy, "I say unto thee, Arise, and take up thy couch, and go into thine house."[13]

Immediately, the man stood, took up the bed upon which he lay, and went to his home, speaking words of praise and adoration to God for the miracle of his healing. The learned men turned and walked away, disgusted and troubled at what Jesus had done.

I had seen Jesus perform other miracles previously, but there was something about the power and light he radiated as he spoke this time. A feeling came over me, one that told me that he had come to do more than just to heal sick bodies. He had come to heal the souls of those who would have the faith to allow him to extend his saving power to them. I had felt his forgiveness. But this power to help us become holy in our nature, even as he was holy, was something that I longed to possess for myself. I had felt this desire before and had repeatedly seen it wane as time passed. I determined that I would follow Jesus the rest of my days so that I might obtain that change in my nature through his power.

The Pharisees continued to try to dishonor Jesus in the eyes of the people. On one occasion Jesus had invited a publican named Levi to come and follow him. Levi was a tax collector for the Roman government, a position despised and hated by Jewish leaders. He was a man of means and invited Jesus and many of his company to come into his home for a feast. Jesus gladly accepted Levi's offer. We sat together and enjoyed a sumptuous meal with Levi and many of his friends.

The Scribes and Pharisees were shocked that Jesus would eat with publicans and sinners. As they murmured amongst themselves and pointed out to some of the disciples exactly with whom Jesus was keeping company, Jesus perceived their thoughts and answered them by saying, "They that are whole need not a physician; but they that are sick. I come not to call the righteous but the sinners to repentance."[14] This only served to further infuriate the Jewish leaders, angry that they could not turn the people against him. Jesus then taught a parable that I am not sure the Pharisees understood, but it helped me to understand why Jesus had come among the poor and lowly in station as my father had foretold.

"No man putteth a piece of new garment upon an old; if otherwise, then both the new maketh a rent, and the piece that was taken out of the new accordeth not with the old. And no man putteth new wine into old bottles; else the new wine will burst the bottles, and be spilled, and the bottles shall perish. But the new wine must be put into new bottles; and both are preserved."[15]

I finally understood that if Jesus had come as a king among the Jewish leaders and tried to teach his gospel of love, forgiveness, and salvation through faith in him rather than through the workings of the law of Moses, it would have burst the bottled-up pride held by the Jews for generations. He would have been rejected and turned away as a lunatic or one who was mad. By coming among the common man, those humble enough to recognize their need for a Savior, he could offer them his redemption, which they would gladly take into their hearts and their lives, filling them with the wine of joy, gladness, and hope.

I felt in my own heart this joy in following Jesus. I felt completely committed and dedicated to him and to his teachings. One morning Jesus came into our camp after he had separated himself from our group for an entire night. He told us that he was going to call twelve special witnesses he referred to as apostles, who would be special witnesses to his name. "To these," he said, "I will give special power to lead and serve the people." When he spoke of a special power, I felt certain that this was the power that I had been seeking. As he spoke, I had the feeling that I would be called as one of these witnesses. Pride began to swell in me as I thought of the special place and calling that I would now have among the people and the power that I would possess.

To my shock and surprise, mine was not among the names he called to serve as one of his apostles. I was stunned. How could he not have chosen me when I had been with him since the beginning? Who could better stand as a witness than me, who had been there on the night of his birth? Instead he had called the fisherman who had just recently joined us. Simon Peter, his brother Andrew, and the two brothers, James and John, were among the first whom he called. He laid his hands upon their heads and ordained them as apostles. He gave each of them a special blessing and power to administer among the people.

He called and ordained Levi, the publican, who was also known as Matthew. He had been with us just a few short weeks. How could he possibly be qualified to stand as a special witness of Jesus as the Christ and Messiah? Yes, they were good men—honest, humble, and sincere in their desires to follow Jesus—but certainly, none could be more qualified to testify of Jesus's divine calling as the Messiah than me. I had heard it proclaimed from heaven by angels! What greater witness and qualifications could one possess?

I was hurt and disappointed when my name wasn't among the group of twelve. Jesus had even called Judas, surnamed Iscariot, whom I detested and despised. He was a shrewd man of business who had joined our group while we had been at one of the feasts in Jerusalem. I felt like he had joined the group simply because he wanted to be among so many who were following Jesus. Certainly, he was not specially qualified to be a witness of the Savior. True, he was good with money and was entrusted with the purse, which was used to purchase supplies for the group as needed, but I did not trust him and could not understand Jesus's care and concern for this man, never mind the fact that he had called him to be an apostle.

I began to wonder if I was just not the caliber of individual whom the Lord required for such a calling. Perhaps there were failings and flaws within me that could just not be overcome or overlooked by the Savior as he chose his leaders. I became sullen and sorrowful over the next couple of days. I noticed that others in our group no longer walked daily with Jesus but had returned to their homes. There were but few who now continued with Jesus other than his twelve apostles. I began to wonder if I, too, should depart and leave the daily labor to those whom he had chosen. I avoided being personally close to Jesus for several days, hoping that he would come to me to explain why he had excluded me from this special calling. After all, I reasoned, did he not owe me some sort of explanation with all that I had gone through and all that I had sacrificed to be with him?

My feelings of disappointment over not having been chosen soon turned to discouragement and doubt that I would ever measure up and be found worthy to obtain the power I sought. I felt a storm raging inside of me. I did not want to become bitter and resentful as I had done before, but I also wasn't willing to let go of my prideful feelings. I felt I deserved to be called. Nor could I ignore the guilt that I felt that perhaps I actually was not worthy or close enough to Jesus to merit his approval. The mix of emotion pulled continually upon my heart and mind and left me outwardly quiet and withdrawn but inwardly churning with thoughts and feelings that I could not seem to control.

One day as we were walking near the Sea of Galilee, Jesus entered into a ship and said, "Let us go over unto the other side of the lake."[16] As we sailed, Jesus fell asleep in the lower portion of the boat. Shortly, there came a terrible storm that began to fill the boat with water and threatened to sink the ship. We all became fearful that we may not survive such a storm. A few of the apostles roused Jesus and cried, "Master, the tempest is raging! How canst thou lie asleep? Save us! Carest thou not that we perish?"

Jesus arose with great calm and peaceful confidence. Looking at the group and then directly at me, he said, "Why are ye so fearful?" He then stretched forth his hand, and with great calm yet with penetrating power in his voice, he said, "Peace! Be still!" Immediately, the winds ceased, the waves became gently calm, and the skies began to clear. Then turning back toward us, he again looked directly at me and said, "How is it ye have no faith?"[17]

The calmness in the waters seemed to wash up over the boat and into my heart. It was as if the storm in me had ceased. Looking into his eyes, I could see that he knew the thoughts and emotions that had raged within me. In that instant I knew again his great love for me, and I also knew that a calling or position did not change that. Later as we finished our journey across the lake, I came quietly to Jesus to once again seek his forgiveness. As he had done before, he grasped my hand and assured me that God was aware of my struggles and was patiently tutoring me to become the man he knew me to be inside. I wanted to ask him why I had not been chosen as one of the twelve, but before I could formulate the question, he said with a peaceful assurance, "Calling and position are not required to serve. Nor do they prove the worth or value of a soul in the kingdom of God. Charity is required to serve your brothers and sisters. True charity allows you to see others and yourself through the eyes with which God sees all his children. Seek unto charity, and you will discover the power that you desire to remain faithful unto the end, for charity never faileth. Remember, faith, hope, and charity and all will be well with you."

Chapter 5

To Touch the Hem

The next several months were filled with miracles and ministrations that caused me to continually marvel at Jesus's power and love for the people. Multitudes from all parts of Galilee came to join in following Jesus. Cheerfully, I walked along with the crowd that continually thronged Jesus. Their joyful mood along with their pressing to be close to him was something that I understood. The crowd now knew that which I had known from his birth. This was no ordinary man with whom we walked, but this was the very Messiah the prophets had said would come and who now moved with might and majesty to minister among the masses. The faltering in my faith from time to time now seemed to be part of a distant past. Since the calming of the sea of Gennesaret, I had contented myself to follow the Master and listen to his teachings, basking in the glow of his spirit and light. I watched and marveled at Jesus's mighty power to calm the water and cause the blind to see, the lame to walk, and the leper to praise God for the miracle of his cleansing. Could anyone not be compelled by his presence to be near him?

Yet while I laughed and celebrated my walk with him, there came one unseen to us all. She moved timidly but determinedly through the pressing crowd. Suffering in silence amid our boisterous banter, she pressed forward from the back of the crowd with unwavering faith in the healing power of the touch of the Master. I gave her no heed, only mindful of my place among my friends, joyfully following Jesus. She pressed between the throng of followers, seeking but to touch the hem of his garment so that she might be made whole. We all bumped and pushed along, often brushing the Savior's robe or grazing his arm as we walked, never imagining that such power could be present in such a touch. Yet she came with a different heart—broken, aching, yearning for the healing that only he could give. In her eyes was a longing for healing, and she willing to pay any price, whatever the sacrifice.

It was this attitude of heart that touched the Savior and brought all of us to an abrupt and silent halt as he asked, "Who touched me?" Simon Peter voiced the question that filled all our minds. "Master, the multitude throng thee and press thee, and sayest thou, Who touched me?"[18] Amid all of the pushing and moving, I had probably touched him a dozen times. Was this what he was asking? Should I admit that I had touched him? I had touched and been touched by Jesus numerous times. I always thought that Jesus was a prophet of the people and that he walked among us because he did not elevate himself as the priests had done. Was he now too good to be touched by those who loved and followed him?

I quickly dismissed the thought because I knew that he was a man of greater love than I had ever known. Then the Savior spoke those words that left me confused and wondering. "I perceive that virtue is gone out of me".[19] As we all stood wondering about his words, she came forward and fell at his feet in sweet adoration and absolute humility, confessing that she had touched him. Still trembling, now with joy as much as fear, she looked questioningly but lovingly into his eyes and told him that she had been healed.

I will never forget the love in his eyes or the kindness in his voice as he raised her to her feet and said gently, "Daughter, be of good comfort: thy faith hath made thee whole; go in peace!"[20] As he lifted her to her feet, I was reminded how I had felt at Jacob's well, but the joy in her face and the light in her countenance told me that she was filled with something that I yet lacked. Her countenance now radiated his light and love and even her walk told me that she was complete, whole, and filled with a peace that I had only felt from him.

As the crowd moved forward, I remained riveted; gazing after the woman, longing to understand what she now possessed. When I had come and emptied myself at his feet at Jacob's well, I remember feeling my burden lifted, but I had not felt the power that I saw in her eyes as Jesus pronounced her whole. Daily, I had walked with him as he opened the scriptures to my understanding, and I felt the divinity of his presence. I had seen his miracles. Yet in one momentary touch, she had gained all that I had hoped would come into my life as I followed Jesus. This was the power that I thought would come if I had only been called as an apostle. Yet I could see in her face and countenance that she now possessed that which I had sought for years, but she had not needed the calling to a high and holy office.

She had now moved out of my view, and I was left alone. For several moments I could not move, wondering what it would take to have what she now possessed. The question began to burn within me, leaving me with no other desire but to know. As I slowly began to move, I did not follow the footsteps of the crowd. I went seeking the woman who had awakened such yearning within me. My searching led me to discover that she had been sick for many years and had spent her entire substance on seeking a cure. She was left broken and alone, having nowhere that she might turn for comfort or relief. Upon hearing of Jesus, she immediately came, having faith that only he could ease her suffering.

I marveled at how blessed she was for having had so heavy a burden as to be drawn to the Savior with such great faith. The grief I had felt had brought me to my knees before Christ, but I had only sought his forgiveness and peace of conscience. I did not realize that he could also give me his power as the woman had received from him. I longed to meet her again, if only to feel that sense of peace that she carried as she left that day. Unfruitful for many days, I decided to give up my quest to find the woman and began to seek again to be among the crowd that followed Jesus.

One day as I was passing along one of the seldom walked streets of Capernaum, I saw her ministering among the poor and the needy. What a filthy, vile people, I thought, wondering why she had come to such a place. Slowly, I approached her, begging her to help me understand. She smiled and invited me to walk with her as she tended among the poor. I could not help but notice the love in her eyes and the tenderness in her voice as she tended to every need—for some a morsel of bread, others a cool cloth on a heated brow, and others simply an ear to hear the longings of their hearts. In each person she touched, I saw a light come to their faces and grateful smiles come to their lips. She was bringing to them what Jesus had given to her.

At the day's end, I sat with her to share a meager meal that she had prepared. I had never partaken of a more satisfying feast. I bid her let me remain that I might help her another day. Without hesitation, she invited me to stay as long as I desired. The days turned into weeks as I tended to those whose needs were so much greater than my own. Oh, that they could but touch the hem of his garment so that they, too, could be healed.

Yet I began to see in their eyes the same light that I had seen come into the woman as she had looked into the face of the Savior. She had brought his light to them, and now even in their great need, there was peace. This was the charity of which Christ had spoken to me after he had calmed my stormy heart. I began to see that I was the one who was truly needy among these humble people. In their humility, I could see the burden of selfishness and pride that enveloped my own heart. I had thought that I was whole because I had no outward ills, but now I could see the issue that had plagued me for these many years. I had focused on my own needs and had sought the blessings of being with Jesus only for myself. I longed to be special above others rather than to see others as my brothers and sisters and to care for their needs.

I ached to have my heart changed and to be made whole. My heart began to break as I realized how much more I needed his healing than these humble people. I desired his healing touch. I longed not just to walk with him but to be one with him that I might love as he loved. My service to these humble people became a labor of love for them, not so much because of their need but because of my need to love, especially those I had wrongfully judged.

I heard that Jesus and his apostles had departed for other cities in the regions of Galilee, yet I remained in Capernaum, working side by side with the woman to help each person find lodging, food, clothing, and medicine.

One day as I was helping to hoe the garden that we had planted, there came a noise and excitement from the street below. Several left the field to go and see. I smiled at their excitement and returned to my hoeing. After several moments I paused to wipe my brow when a voice said, "Well done, thou good and faithful servant."[21] Looking toward the sun, I could not clearly see his face, but his gentle voice pierced me as never before in my walk with him. I fell immediately to my face, grateful but to touch the hem of his garment. Calling me by name, he raised me to my feet as I gazed into those kind and loving eyes. Piercing me through to my very center, he uttered words that sang sweet music to my soul and brought a peace that I had never known. "Inasmuch as ye have done it unto one of the least of these my brethren, ye have done it unto me.[22] Thy sins are forgiven the. Go in peace."[23]

From that moment on, I no longer needed to be among the jostling crowd, clamoring to see the miracles. I have witnessed instead the miracle of his virtuous power as it enters into the hearts of his children. I finally came to understand that charity is the pure love of Christ; not just love for him or from him but like him. As I have reflected on his great love for me, I have felt no other desire than to share that love with others so that they, too, might come to feel his love and love him as I have come to love him.

I have become a true witness that those who seek him and serve their fellowman with all their heart, might, mind, and strength will find healing and peace that passes all understanding. They will be possessed of charity until they become like him, not just in doing as he does but in loving as he loves. This love purifies the motives of the heart and moves a person to help others, not out of self-interest for recognition or reward but simply because it has become one's nature to love and serve others so that others may also come to know God and feel his love for them. A person possessed of charity simply becomes a conduit of God's love.

Chapter 6

Feasting

As I served among the people of Capernaum, not only did I come to know and love them, but I also came to greatly admire the woman who had led me to this place. She was possessed of true charity. I came not only to admire her but to love her. Our work together served to knit our hearts in love. I sought to spend as much time with her as possible. I learned that she was from a wealthy family in Jerusalem and had married well in her social class. She and her husband had moved to Capernaum, where he had a thriving business. When she had become ill and was unable to have children, her husband divorced her, but he had left her with the house and money to live. She had exhausted most of her resources in seeking a cure for her disease. She had lost hope and had fallen into despair. I well understood all that she had felt in her time of need.

She told me that a challenge even greater than her illness was the bitterness that she felt inside of her because of the many disappointments that she had had to face in her life. All she had wanted was to be a mother and to serve her children. This had not been possible, and then it had cost her her marriage. Her bitterness had caused her to turn away from others who had tried to help her, including her family. The real issue that plagued her had become her anger. This caused her health to worsen. Her physical body began to reflect the inner pain that she felt. She lost all hope of ever finding happiness or joy in her life. Instead of seeking to serve, she had turned inward in self-pity and hopelessness.

Then she had heard news of Jesus going among the people, healing and helping all in need. Almost involuntarily, hope began to grow inside of her. She realized that she must come to the Savior not just to be physically healed but to have the bitterness removed and to regain her righteous desires to forget herself and serve others. It was this deep yearning for complete healing—both body and spirit—that moved her to find the Savior. She could not with words describe what had taken place in her when Jesus had pronounced her whole; however, tears filled her eyes as she looked into mine, and I knew. She then said something that rang so profoundly in my heart that I immediately felt the truth sink deep into every fiber of my soul. "I have found that as long as I allowed bitterness to fill my cup, there was little room for love. But once I allowed the Savior's love to fill me, all bitterness was gone, and I felt whole and able to love in the way that he loved me."

In one small phrase, she had articulated what had overwhelmed me in the moment I saw her healed by Jesus and what was happening inside of me as I served others. It was his love being manifested through me to them. All resentment or bitterness for past injustices seemed to dissipate like the morning mist fleeing before the rising sun. Once I let the Son of God into my heart and began to live with the love that he had shown me, I could not return to who or what I was before.

I shared my past with her—my business, my wife's passing, and my joy in finding Jesus. I spoke of my experience at the manger, my time with Jesus as a boy, and then my struggle to live what he had taught me. I informed her that I was half Samaritan. I knew and felt the injustice placed upon me by others. I shared that I had also felt the pain of loss that had filled my heart with grief to the point where I was unable to feel God's love for me. I spoke of the feelings that had come to me after witnessing her being healed by the touch of the Master. I told her of my longing for that power to come into my life by such a touch. I shared with her the realization of that longing as I served with her among the poor.

I also informed her that I was currently a man without means but that I would still treasure the privilege of spending time with her. She smiled and told me that my companionship meant more to her than silver or gold. We continued to serve among the poor, while I also found work in the local markets. The owner of the shop where I worked allowed me to sleep in a small room in the back of the shop. Soon I began saving money so that I would be able to seek my newfound friend's hand in marriage. We pursued our relationship, and we planned to wed in the spring.

My wife's family traveled the long journey to attend the wedding. Though quite wealthy, to my pleasant surprise, I found her parents to be very humble people. I was at first concerned that they would not accept one who was part Samaritan, but they welcomed me into their family with warmth, tenderness, and love. Evidently, their daughter had written to them regarding the healing that she had experienced through Jesus's power and told them of one of his disciples who had for several weeks been giving of himself tirelessly in helping her to care for those in need. I was a bit embarrassed by their praise and gratitude, but I was grateful for their acceptance. I quickly came to love them as my own parents. They invited us to join them in Jerusalem for the Passover feast, and we gratefully accepted their offer.

I had not been to Jerusalem to celebrate Passover since the days when I had shared my tent with Jesus so many years before. The city was abuzz with people for the celebration. My new father-in-law was a man who trafficked in textiles in Jerusalem, and they lived in a very nice home not far from the center of the city. I felt an excitement growing within me as the festival and the feast approached. This would be the first time that I had fully participated in Passover since I had gained my newfound faith and understanding of the Savior. I was anxious to see the feast through the new eyes of my conversion.

My in-laws had heard about Jesus through the writings of their daughter, but had not heard him preach nor seen his miracles. I shared with them my previous experiences with Jesus and testified that he was God's only begotten Son, who was sent to save the world from sin. I explained that our Passover lamb was a symbol of Jesus as the Lamb of God. They seemed interested, but I could tell that there was much they still questioned. They were much steeped in the traditions of the Jews, and many of their friends held prominent positions among the Sanhedrin. It was difficult for them to rethink so much of what they had been taught regarding the Messiah, but they were willing to listen and sought to understand our teachings about Jesus.

Despite the challenges faced in trying to teach my in-laws, the symbolism of the Passover touched me deeply. The blood on the doorposts, the unleavened bread, and the prayers of praise and thanksgiving all seemed to humble me and prepare me to be taught. As I ate of the bitter herbs that represented Israel's bondage, I could not help but think of my own bitterness, which before had caused me to turn away from God. I realized now the lasting bondage and bitter effects of sin. As I ate the herbs, I longed for something to take away the bitter taste. As the wine passed through my lips following the herbs, I marveled at its sweetness and the immediate removal of the bitterness of the herbs. I thought about the sweet feeling I received when Jesus had embraced me near Jacob's well. I felt the living water that he had promised the woman who had brought the message of his coming to our city. His embrace removed my bitterness as quickly and completely as the wine had removed the taste of the herbs from my mouth.

As we progressed through the various parts of the Passover, I noticed that occasionally the bitterness of the herbs would return. It was not until I had partaken of the lamb that the aftertaste from the herbs was completely removed. As I contemplated this experience, I thought about the times when I had allowed my own bitterness to return to me, even after feeling the Savior's sweet embrace. It was not until I had begun to serve others as he had served me that I felt the continual power and peace that he had promised. In that moment, I understood that only as I take the Savior into the way that I live my life day to day can the effects of sin be completely removed from my life. I determined that I would continue to follow the Savior and serve others throughout my life so that I might continually feel a remission of my sins.

Up until this point, I had not realized that Christ had come not only to remove sin but to also bring me to be at one with God. Little did I know at the time the sacrifice that would be required to refine me and allow me to experience the purifying and perfecting process necessary to become all that he saw in me.

Chapter 7

Manna from Heaven

Following the feast, my father-in-law asked about my work in the markets of Capernaum. I told him that I was not much more than a shop boy. I intended to work hard to advance my position to enable me to care for his daughter. I told him of my past business experience and assured him that I knew what it would take to regain my wealth and position. He seemed pleased and asked if I would be willing to help him expand his textile business into Capernaum. He told me that he could provide me the means to purchase a shop and then would supply me with the material to begin my business. I was elated at the opportunity to care for my wife and provide her with a more comfortable living. We settled upon an agreement of my wages, and he supplied me with a caravan to carry the supplies back to Capernaum. I felt blessed that the Lord had opened the way for me to regain that which I had lost. After I told my wife about her father's offer, we knelt together to thank the Lord for his goodness and mercy toward us.

Upon our return to Capernaum, I busied myself with getting the new business underway. We were extremely blessed by the Lord, and soon our business was providing more than a modest living. For almost a year, I labored diligently in the markets to increase the business and once again enjoyed the fruits of wealth. Often I would hear people in the market talk about Jesus, who continued to preach throughout the land of Galilee. I did not travel daily with him, but I sought diligently to listen to him whenever he preached near enough that I could attend without losing any business.

On one occasion, my wife and I journeyed across the Sea of Galilee to the small town of Bethsaida to hear the Savior preach. I recalled this place from the time when Jesus had called Peter and his brother into his service. Jesus healed many people and preached words that brought hope and joy to our hearts as we listened well into the afternoon. As the evening approached, we did not want to leave, but we had not eaten the entire day while we were listening to Jesus. We were about to depart when Jesus bid us to stay. I saw him discussing something with one of the apostles. Then it happened.

A young boy brought forth a small basket in which he had a few loaves of bread and a couple of small fish. I began to wonder how Jesus planned to feed such a multitude with so little. He invited us to sit down. He then broke the bread and blessed it. I was reminded of my experience sharing a meal with him as a twelve-year-old boy. His prayer seemed to pierce the heavens and invoke blessings that filled our souls. He gave some of the bread and fish to the apostles, who then distributed it among the people. Unexplainably, the bread and fish continued to fill each basket that the Savior sent forth until every person had been fed. I did not know exactly how many people had eaten, but I knew that it was more than a few loaves and fishes could have possibly fed. As I partook of the meal provided by the miraculous power of Jesus, I realized that it was not just my body that was full. It was my heart and soul. Never had so little filled so many, yet I was a witness to the complete absence of hunger that followed such a feast. Overwhelmed at this miracle, some of the people sought to take Jesus and make him a king. Jesus refused, but the crowd clamored to enforce their desires. At this, Jesus turned and departed from the crowd, seeking time to be alone.

Night was coming on, and we needed passage back across the sea to Capernaum. I sought out Peter to see if my wife and I might join them in their ship. When Peter saw me, he embraced me as a brother. I felt the change that had come upon him during his time with Jesus. I could see why the Savior had chosen him to lead the apostles. He gladly welcomed us aboard the ship, and we made our way across the lake as the sun set behind the hills, leaving only traces of light lingering in the sky.

During our journey, a storm began to blow across the lake. Soon we were unable to make any headway toward the shore at Capernaum. I helped the men row most of the night without much progress. We rowed into the fourth watch, and we had become exhausted. We lacked the strength to continue rowing. Suddenly, we saw a man coming toward the ship, walking out upon the water. One of the disciples called out in fear, "It is a spirit!" Most of the disciples began to fear, but I felt a calming peace within me. I stepped to the edge of the boat, straining to see through the darkness. Then came words that I had heard before. "Be of good cheer!" I remembered back to the days of my youth when an angel had spoken similar words of comfort out on the plains of Bethlehem. Though he was still not completely visible, Jesus spoke words that brought calm to the troubled hearts of the apostles. "It is I. Be not afraid."

Peter joined me at the edge of the boat and said, "Lord, if it be thou, bid me come unto thee on the water." Jesus responded with one simple word, "Come."[24]

I stood motionless as Peter climbed over the bow of the ship. I marveled at his faith and courage to step out onto a stormy sea. To my amazement, he began to walk upon the water to the Savior. After taking several steps upon the water, I saw him hesitate. I saw fear arise in his eyes as he began to focus upon the waves and turbulent waters beneath him. He no longer focused upon the Master but instead began to sink into the depths of his own fear and doubt. As he sank farther and farther into the water, he cried out, "Lord, save me!" Immediately, Jesus stretched forth his hand and lifted Peter from the depths of his doubt and despair. As he put his arm around Peter he said gently, "O thou of little faith, wherefore didst thou doubt?"[25]

The words rang deep in my soul, knowing that I, too, had doubted in my times of distress. I marveled that Peter had had the faith and courage to even step out of the boat. With such faith, I began to wonder why he had begun to sink. I knew that his faith in the Savior was strong, for in his need, he still appealed to Jesus for help, knowing his power to save. Why had he begun to sink when he had such faith in Christ? As I pondered this thought, I felt as if I was searching my own soul to understand why I had repeatedly sunk into my own despair when I had faced the struggles of life.

As we approached the shore and the morning sun crested the horizon, light also came into my mind, and I realized that Peter, like me, had lost sight of the Savior and focused instead upon the difficulty of the challenge. Just as the sun chased away the darkness and fears of the night, I realized that keeping my eye on the Son of God can give to me the courage not only to get out of the boat but to stay above the winds and the waves of life that seek to bring me down. It then occurred to me that Peter had walked upon the water to return to the boat! By taking the Savior's hand, he was again able to walk upon the water and overcome his doubt in his own lack of ability. He simply trusted in the Savior to give him strength to overcome whatever obstacle was in his path. This newfound vision warmed my soul like the rays of the morning sun warmed the chill of the previous night out on the sea.

The day following, many people came into Capernaum and sought Jesus. They asked him how he had arrived on this side of the lake, seeing that he had not entered a boat the night before. This Jesus did not address but instead spoke to the reason they had come. "Ye seek me not because ye desire to keep my sayings, neither because ye saw the miracles, but because ye did eat of the loaves, and were filled. Labor not for the meat which perisheth, but for that meat which endureth unto everlasting life, which the Son of man shall give unto you: for him hath God the Father sealed."[26]

I could tell that many were confused by his words. I heard one man say to another alongside him, "If he were really a prophet, would he not give us daily bread as Moses provided the manna in the wilderness?"

As if reading his thoughts, Jesus answered, "Moses gave you not that bread from heaven; but my Father giveth you the true bread from heaven. For the bread of God is he which cometh down from heaven, and giveth life unto the world."[27] Excited by the idea of receiving heavenly bread, the multitude exclaimed, "Lord, evermore give us this bread."[28]

Jesus then replied with words that resonated with power and truth. "I am the Bread of Life: he that cometh to me shall never hunger; and he that believeth on me shall never thirst."[29] I was beginning to understand. Jesus was here to provide us the things that would feed our souls, not just our bellies. Many, however, continued to murmur and disbelieve. How had his Father sent him to be the Bread of Life for the world? Was not this the son of Joseph and Mary, whom they had known from his youth? How was he to be the Bread of Life and give them bread from heaven? The questions swirled through the crowd like the wind blowing leaves around the shores of the lake.

Jesus then spoke boldly, "I am the Bread of Life. Your fathers did eat manna in the wilderness, and are dead. This is the bread which cometh down from heaven, that a man may eat thereof, and not die. I am the living bread which came down from heaven: if any man eat of this bread, he shall live forever: and the bread that I will give is my flesh, which I will give for the life of the world."[30]

"How is this possible?" I asked myself. I understood that his words were like manna to my soul, but how could he give me his flesh that I might not taste of death? Amidst my confusion, Jesus then said, "Except ye eat the flesh of the Son of man, and drink his blood, ye have no life in you. Whoso eateth my flesh and drinketh my blood, hath eternal life; and I will raise him up in the resurrection of the just at the last day. For my flesh is meat indeed, and my blood is drink indeed. He that eateth my flesh, and drinketh my blood, dwelleth in me, and I in him."[31]

I was now even more confused. I had seen Jesus perform miracles.

My mind had been illuminated by his words of transcendent light. I had felt the love of his embrace. But my mind was now in a fog. How could he give me his flesh as manna from heaven? How was I to drink his blood? The thought was repulsive! Surely, this had to be some sort of symbolic representation.

As I pondered and wondered at his words, thoughts of the Passover came into my mind and brought blazing light of understanding into my heart. Had the wine not been a representation of his blood? Had I not felt enlightened and enlivened as I partook of his blood? Had the bitterness of my sins not been removed as I partook of the lamb, which represented this man who now stood boldly proclaiming himself to be sent from God to save us? I wept with joy at the thought of this manna that the Lord had sent. I also wept at the idea that Jesus would have to die in order to bring to pass my opportunity to become like him and enjoy eternal life with my Father in heaven. I marveled at Jesus's love and willingness to sacrifice himself for me as well as those who stood murmuring and doubting.

I looked to my wife to share with her what I was feeling and saw that she, too, had tears streaming down her face. In just a look, we both knew what the other knew. We embraced and felt the joy of Jesus's teachings penetrate deep into our hearts.

Our feelings were not shared by the people standing about us. I could hear their murmuring and doubts about what Jesus had taught. "This is a hard saying," I heard one man say. Knowing the growing discontent among his followers, Jesus asked, "Doth this offend you? It is the spirit that quickeneth; the flesh profiteth nothing: the words that I speak unto you, they are spirit, and they are life."[32]

I felt the Spirit that Jesus had described. It brought light and understanding that seemed to penetrate deep into my soul so that I could understand and also comprehend his sayings. It was obvious that many in the crowd did not share this enlightenment from the Spirit.

Disappointed that there was to be no bread, disgruntled at his sayings, and disdaining the thought of eating his flesh and drinking his blood, many of those who had come to see Jesus departed. I could see in their eyes that they had lost their desire to follow a man who spoke such confusing and difficult words. I ached to help them understand, but I found myself afraid to speak. They seemed determined to walk no more after Jesus.

If only they could understand, I thought. I realized in my own heart that until one has sought to understand by the Spirit, one cannot hope to comprehend the truth and light of the Savior's teachings. The manna that had been sent to Israel out in the wilderness, designed by God to point all to Christ, had only served to fill the bellies of the wandering ancient Israelites and fill with confusion the minds of those who now sought only for the physical bread. They could not see the symbolism of the Savior's life and mission. By seeking the physical bread, which only served to sustain life temporarily, they had missed the manna sent from heaven, even God's own Son, who would give himself to provide life that would go on forever.

Chapter 8

Bearing Witnesses and Crosses

My wife and I were standing close by Peter as many of the multitude departed. I saw Jesus turn toward his apostles and asked with a sadness that I could feel, "Will ye also go away?"

Peter stepped forward, looked into the Savior's eyes, and said boldly, "Lord, to whom shall we go? Thou hast the words of eternal life."[33] Jesus reached out and put his hand upon Peter's shoulder. He smiled and then turned to the other apostles and asked, "Whom say the people that I am?" They responded, "Some say thou art John the Baptist, others say thou art Elias, and yet others believe that thou art Jeremias or old prophets that are risen again."[34]

Visibly saddened, Jesus turned away in silence, looking off toward the horizon. Then turning back toward the apostles and looking deeply into the eyes of each, he asked quietly, "But whom say ye that I am?"[35] The question seemed to pierce my soul. Though not an apostle, I had witnessed many of the miracles of Jesus. I knew in my heart that he was more than a man. I had felt the power of the Passover witness to me that he was the Lamb of God. I ached to tell what I knew, but I felt timid in my testimony.

As I was filled with these thoughts, Peter stepped forward and answered with a boldness that was typical of his conviction, "Thou art the Christ, the Son of the living God!"

Jesus then looked upon Peter, embraced him, and said, "Blessed art thou, Simon, Bar-jona, for flesh and blood hath not revealed it unto thee, but my Father which is in heaven. And I say also unto thee that thou art Peter, and upon this rock I will build my church; and the gates of hell shall not prevail against it. And I will give unto thee the keys of the kingdom of heaven: and whatsoever that shalt bind on earth shall be bound in heaven: and whatsoever thou shalt loose on earth, shall be loosed in heaven."[36]

As Peter's witness and the Savior's blessing for such a witness sounded in my ears, I wondered why I was not able to speak boldly the things I knew and understood. I certainly knew that Jesus was the Christ, yet I found myself without the courage to declare what I knew to be true. Perhaps this was the reason that I had not been asked by the Savior to serve as one of his special witnesses. I realized in my heart that knowing is not enough. I must be willing to share what I know with others so that they, too, might gain a witness of Jesus and his mission.

As I pondered these ideas, Jesus spoke of his coming mission and the events that lay ahead for him. "The Son of man must suffer many things, and be rejected of the elders and chief priests and scribes, and be slain, and be raised the third day."

Peter turned and took hold of Jesus and said, "Be it far from thee, Lord: this shall not be unto thee."

Jesus broke free of Peter's grasp and said, "Get thee behind me Satan: thou art an offense unto me: for thou savourest not the things that be of God, but those that be of men."[37]

I was stunned at the Savior's response to Peter, whom moments before he had embraced and blessed. How is it that one of such true conviction and testimony of the Savior could be thus rebuked and chastened publicly? I was grateful that I had not spoken but had held my peace when Jesus had said that he would have to die. I knew from my experience with the Passover that Jesus had come to give his life, but to hear him speak openly of his death left me desiring for it not to be so. I wondered how these things were to be and how we were to follow a man who spoke of his own demise and who seemed so resigned to readily give up his life.

As if to read my thoughts, the Savior said, "If any man will come after me, let him deny himself, and take up his cross daily, and follow me. For whosever will save his life shall lose it: but whosever will lose his life for my sake, the same shall save it." Then turning as if to speak directly to me, he said, "For what is a man advantaged, if he gain the whole world, and lose himself, or be cast away? For whosoever shall be ashamed of me and of my words, of him shall the Son of man be ashamed when he shall come in his own kingdom, clothed in the glory of his Father, with the holy angels."[38]

Once again, I felt the foundations of my soul being shaken. Deny myself and take up my cross? What cross was I to take up to follow him? Was I to lose my life and die for him? Is that what he expected of me? How could a person lose his life in order to save it? As times before, I was confused at his words. I knew that I could never be ashamed of the Savior, but what was he now asking of me that I was not willing to give? I had faithfully followed his teachings and served others with love and kindness. I had sought to live honestly and compassionately among my fellow man, but now it seemed as if he were asking me to give my very life for him.

I turned to my wife and noticed that she was riveted by the Savior, absorbing every word. I gently touched her on the arm, and she turned to me with a smile. I suggested we return home before it became too dark. As we began to make our way home, my mind seemed to be as confused and twisted as the streets of the city. My wife sensed my questioning and troubled heart. She asked me if everything was okay. I expressed to her my lack of understanding of what the Savior was asking of us.

With loving understanding, my wife explained that Jesus seeks that we all become complete and whole by receiving all that the Father has to give us. In order for us to receive all that the Father has for us, we must be willing to empty ourselves of our own self-centered thoughts and concerns. She said that it is much like a glass of water. As long as we are filled with that which we put into the glass, there is not room for the things that the Lord desires to place in us that we may become one with him. Only as we deny ourselves of all the worldly self-concerns that take us away from God can we be sufficiently open to receive the Spirit and the living waters of the Lord.

We walked the rest of the journey home in silence, my mind racing to understand what Jesus and my wife had spoken. I wondered what I had yet to give in order to be an open vessel for the Lord to fill. I continued to try to convince myself that my service, my love, and my conviction of Jesus as the Christ were sufficient, yet deep inside, I knew that I still had doubts that I could completely give my heart, my soul, and my life to him.

Chapter 9

Prosperity and Parables

The next few months, I filled my life with the dealings of my shop and business. Sales of the textiles soared, and my father-in-law seemed very pleased. He made me a partner in the business and gave me full run of the shop in Capernaum. I felt that I was finally able to provide for my wife the comforts of life that she deserved. While my wife sought to listen to the Savior whenever he was close by, my time and energy were spent more and more with the store. Soon it seemed that there was time for little else.

As fall approached, our shop was on the verge of tremendous expansion, and we needed much more material. I contacted my father-in-law, and he suggested that we come to Jerusalem for the Feast of Tabernacles. Then we could carry more cloth back with us to Capernaum. Anxious to enjoy the feast in the city, we packed our belongings for the journey. My wife told me she had heard that Jesus, too, would be attending the feast and asked if we could join with his group in making the journey to Jerusalem. I hesitantly agreed, knowing I had yet to face the unanswered questions from my last meeting with Jesus.

Deep in my heart, I knew that I had allowed the shop to consume much of my time to avoid dealing with the troubling idea that I yet lacked something in my discipleship of Christ. I had contented myself with the idea that I was a good person who had accepted my need for Christ in my life. I continued to reach out to the poor and continued to serve others in my community. I had not fallen into any grievous sins and had truly tried to live all that Jesus taught. I attended the synagogue weekly, read daily from the Torah, fasted regularly, and sought God daily and diligently in prayer. I remembered the Savior's words to not get angry with my brother, to fast privately not publicly, and to stay away from thoughts that were impure and unholy. I tried not to judge others unrighteously, but I sought diligently to build my life upon the teachings of Jesus. Surely, this was all that I could do to give my life to him. Yet deep inside, something nagged at me. I felt that there was more that I could give, that I was still holding back a part of my heart.

In walking the journey with Jesus to Jerusalem, I felt once again the love and concern he showed for each individual. All along the journey, Jesus took time to teach and to heal those who would come unto him. As we passed through the area of Samaria, however, there were those who would not receive him. Some of the apostles were incensed that the people would reject him, and they implored the Savior to send retribution upon the people. Jesus tenderly but firmly rebuked them by saying, "Ye know not what manner of spirit ye are of. For the Son of man is not come to destroy men's lives, but to save them."[39]

Not come to destroy? But had he not said that we must lose our lives for him? Again, the questions began to tug at my heart and occupy my mind. How was I to lose my life for him? I observed as others came who desired to follow Jesus. Each seemed to have good reasons why they could not leave everything to follow him. I felt as if each of them was facing questions similar to what I was experiencing. How was his asking me to lose my life for him his way of saving me?

As we were nearing Jerusalem, one man approached Jesus and asked, "Master, what shall I do to inherit eternal life?" Immediately, I gave my full attention, seeking to know this truth for myself.

The Savior responded by asking the man, "What is written in the law? How readest thou?"

The man responded in much the same way in which I would have answered. "Thou shalt love the Lord thy God with all thy heart, and with all thy soul, and with all thy strength, and with all thy mind: and thy neighbor as thyself."

Jesus answered him, "Thou hast answered right: this do and thou shalt live."

The man then asked a question in an attempt to justify himself, "And who is my neighbor?"[40]

As the Savior responded to the man, he looked my direction and said, "A certain man went down from Jerusalem to Jericho, and fell among thieves, which stripped him of his raiment, and wounded him, and departed, leaving him half dead. And by chance there came down a certain priest that way: and when he saw him, he passed by on the other side. And likewise, a Levite, when he was at the place, came and looked on him, and passed by on the other side. But a certain Samaritan, as he journeyed, came where he was: and when he saw him, he had compassion on him, and went to him, and bound up his wounds, pouring in oil and wine, and set him on his own beast, and brought him to an inn, and took care of him. And on the morrow when he departed, he took out two pence, and gave them to the host, and said unto him, Take care of him; and whatsoever thou spendest more, when I come again, I will repay thee." Jesus then asked the man, "Which now of these three, thinkest thou, was neighbor unto him that fell among the thieves?"

The man answered, "He that shewed mercy on him."

Then said Jesus unto him, "Go, and do thou likewise."[41]

As the man departed, the rest of the crowd marveled at the wisdom of Jesus's response, but I sat stunned and confused. I knew the story that he had told all too well. How did he know what I had done so many years before? Why did he tell this story when he knew that I was listening? It was as if he wanted me to know that he knew.

Humbled and confused, I waited until the crowd had departed before I timidly approached the Savior and explained my confusion over his teachings. Why had he used me as an example when I had such questions about losing my life for his sake? Surely, if he knew my dealings with Luke so many years before, he knew of my questions and my doubts about my own discipleship.

In the quiet of a solitary moment, one-on-one with the Savior, he looked deep into my eyes and said, "Thy Father, which seeth in secret, will reward thee openly. These many years ye have sought to faithfully follow, and yet ye have doubted thine own discipleship. Rememberest thou Peter upon the water?" I nodded. "Peter sank not because of his lack of faith in me but because he doubted his own ability to follow me. His focus turned to himself and his doubts rather than to his faith in me."

"Thou hast many times left the boat of thine own making and sought to come unto me upon the waters of life, only to lose sight of thy faith. Doubt not thy faith, dear brother, but doubt thy doubts. Did I not say unto thee, 'Well done thou good and faithful servant?' In thee I have seen great love and service, but I have also seen thy fear to leave all doubt behind and walk confidently in the strength of my love for thee. Do not take counsel from thy fears. Dwell not upon thy faults; forget thyself and remember that my grace is sufficient to make thy weaknesses become strengths if thou wilt but humble thyself and have faith in my ability to make thee strong. Ye need not fear, for I am with thee. Thou took me in as a child in Jerusalem, and hast sought all of thy days to live my teachings. Cast not away thy confidence because thy steps at times falter. I knowest thy heart. As thou hast sought to follow me, repent quickly when thou stumblest, and know that I will cover all thy sins with a cloak of mercy, forgiveness, and love."

The Savior went silent as I sat weeping before him. I had felt his love many times in the years since I had kissed him as a babe in the manger, but never had I sensed his confidence in the person I was becoming. As I looked up to gaze into his eyes, they became as a mirror in which I was able to see the person I had always wanted to be. He had never lost sight of that vision of me, and now he was showing me who I was to become if I would stop worrying about myself and simply serve others out of love. I realized that I still had steps to go along that journey, but now I felt and sensed with all my soul who I was to be.

Sitting silently before the Savior, I pleaded in my heart that I would never lose sight of that vision, even during the times when I stumbled. Knowing my thoughts and the longings in my heart, Jesus embraced me and said gently, "Even in the times when thou dost forget, yet will I not forget thee. I will engraven thee upon the palms of my hands so that thou mayest know my love and become all that I have shown unto thee."

The deep meaning and import of his words slipped passed me at the time of his telling them to me. All I knew was that his words left me filled with greater joy than I had ever known. I finally realized that Jesus did not love me because I was perfect in my obedience but because he saw me as his brother and child of our Father, who loved us both. I no longer needed to be perfect to feel that I merited his love. I simply needed to go forward in faith, loving my brothers and sisters and striving to do his will and the will of our Father, trusting in his ability to make me perfect. I felt a great burden lifted from me as I emptied myself of my own feelings of inadequacy and self-doubt and accepted the Savior's yoke of faith and trust in him.

Chapter 10

Love, Light, and Living Water

When I returned to my wife, she immediately knew that something had changed in me. She embraced me and invited me to share what I had experienced with the Savior. I could not hold back the emotions that filled my heart as I told her the sacred things Jesus had shared with me. My love for the Savior seemed to fill my entire being, and I felt his love flow through me and outward toward all people. I could not bear the thought of anyone not knowing and feeling the Savior's love for them. I no longer felt timid about testifying that Jesus was not only the Messiah but also the Savior of all mankind. With all my soul, I desired to share this love and message with every person I knew. My wife understood, and we rejoiced in the love which Jesus offered to us and to all people.

As we entered the city for the feast, my wife and I bid farewell to Jesus and made our way to the home of her family. We were excited to share with them the wonderful message of the Savior. While we had talked with them before about Jesus and what he had done, we felt compelled this time to help them not just understand his teachings but to feel his love for them.

When we arrived at their home, we saw that they had several guests with them. We learned that most of them were members of the Sanhedrin. They were discussing Jesus and the many rumors that were circulating around the city regarding him. My wife's parents seemed more curious than ever to meet this Jesus and see for themselves this man who caused such a division among the people. Some professed him to be a prophet, while others denounced him as a fraud. My in-laws had told their friends that we not only knew Jesus but had spent many hours with him and could inform them about who he really was.

After we had unpacked our things, we were invited to visit with them regarding our dealings with Jesus. Anxiously, we began to share our witness of Jesus and the fact that he was indeed the long-awaited Messiah. It became quickly apparent that our parents' guests did not agree.

They smiled at our ignorance and gullible acceptance of a mere carpenter as the chosen Messiah. They haughtily cited from the Torah and Talmud that the Messiah would be a great king who would come to rule upon the earth with power, might, and vengeance upon the wicked. They explained how he would throw off the yoke of Roman bondage from the Jewish people and reign supreme upon the earth. With a self-knowing and arrogant air, they inquired, "And how do you expect this simple carpenter—from Nazareth no less—to achieve such a victory?"

We tried to explain to them how Jesus would throw off the yoke of bondage by showing us the true love that God has for each of his children. We told of the miracles that Jesus had wrought—walking upon the water, causing the storm to cease, and healing all manner of disease and forgiving sins among the people. We tried to share with them our feelings of his great love, but they just smiled and shook their heads at our childlike belief in such an "obvious imposter," as they called him. Feeling the futility of our attempts, we humbly shared with them our witness of what we knew to be true, but the Spirit of our testimony fell like a hammer against the anvil of their hardened hearts.

Seeing that they would not deter us from our belief, they arose to leave. They thanked their hosts for their hospitality, exchanged the pleasantries of parting, and left for their own dwellings. After they had departed, our parents began to question us further.

They were worried that we had been taken in by a man who was pretending to be something that he was not. We reminded them of the great healing that he had done for their daughter, but they were not convinced that this miraculous gift made him the awaited Messiah.

"We are sure that he is a good man who is doing some wonderful things," they said. "But do you really believe that he is the one chosen of God to save our people?" We assured them that Jesus was indeed the Messiah and that he would save the people but not in the way they expected. We explained that he had come to save the people from the oppression of their own sin and selfishness. He had come to show us how to live with love for one another. We shared with them the great witness of his love, which we had gained for ourselves during our walk with him.

As we spoke into the night, we could see that their hearts were beginning to soften, especially as we shared with them our personal experiences in feeling the Savior's love. The Spirit of truth confirmed our words in their hearts, but they still had reservations about changing their lives based upon our witness. They desired to see and know for themselves that Jesus was indeed the promised Messiah. We encouraged them to pray to God that they might know for themselves. They agreed.

As we prepared for our evening prayer, I asked if I might be permitted to offer prayer. My father-in-law was a bit reluctant, as it was the tradition for the head of the household to recite the prayer, but with encouragement from his wife and daughter, he agreed. I did not recite the typical evening prayer from the Talmud, but instead I spoke with God with all the feeling of my heart. The Spirit gave me utterance as I thanked God for his love and kindness and for the goodness of the hearts of my in-laws. I prayed that they might be blessed with the Spirit to know for themselves of the things of which we had testified. I thanked God for his Son, whom he had sent among us to teach us how to live so that we might know and feel his love for us. I closed my prayer in the name of Jesus, the Messiah and Son of God.

Following the prayer, there was silence, except for the soft sobbing of my wife and mother-in-law. My wife gently placed her arm around the shoulder of her mother, and they embraced. My father-in-law had not yet raised his head. After several moments, he raised his eyes to meet mine. With a sincere longing in his eyes, he asked, "Do you really believe that Jesus is the very Son of God?"

"I not only believe it," I replied. "I know it through the power and witness of the Holy Spirit."

"Is that what I am feeling?" he asked. "Is this the Spirit of the Lord speaking to my heart?" I assured him that it was. His head quickly bowed again as if he were praying silently to God. I quietly placed my hand on his shoulder and could feel him beginning to shake as he sought to fight back the tears. His wife reached over and took his hands. I moved over by my wife and put my arm around her. My father-in-law finally looked up into the eyes of his dear companion, and they fell into each other's arms, sobbing. We stood in silence, tears in our eyes as we smiled at the marvelous scene that had unfolded before us.

Surely, this was what the Savior meant when he had asked me to lose my life for him. It was no longer about me, about whether or not I was measuring up to all the expectations I put upon myself. It was now about sharing with others Jesus's great love and the importance of his life and mission. It was now about bringing others to him, not simply about my own obedience and striving to live his gospel. Once I had felt his love and his confidence in who I was to become, my only thought and desire was to help all of God's children know the Father through the love, life, and mission of Jesus.

The following days we attended the celebrations and ceremonies of the Feast of Tabernacles with my in-laws. The week of the feast seemed so much more meaningful to me with the new understandings that I had gained in my journey with Jesus. I had always been impressed by the magnificent candelabras that were set in the center square and illuminated the entire city during the feast. One could not help but look upward and gaze upon these amazing lights. But this time as I gazed upon their brilliance, they seemed to be illuminating more than just the city. They brought to my mind what Jesus had taught in one of his sermons. We were to be the light of the world, and we are to make our light shine so that others could glorify God.

As I pondered about how the candelabras allowed me to see through the darkness, it struck me that I had shared the light I had gained about the Savior with my in-laws so that they could see through the darkness of the traditions of their friends. I had seen their hearts and minds fill with light, and now they glorified God and worshipped Jesus as the Messiah. We continued to teach my in-laws each evening as we returned from the festivities. They truly seemed to understand and enjoy the messages of truth we shared.

Each morning we went to witness the priest draw waters from the pool of Siloam and pour the waters into the basins within the temple. This scene had once been described to me as the true essence of joy and rejoicing. While I found it enjoyable, it did not hold the same joy for me that I had felt in being with Jesus, but I tried to understand to some degree the sacred nature of the event.

On the last day of the feast, in the quiet, sacred moment of the pouring of the water, to the shock and surprise of everyone, including me, Jesus stood up and said with a loud voice, "If any man thirst, let him come unto me, and drink. He that believeth on me, as the scripture hath said, out of his belly shall flow rivers of living water."[42]

At first, I was a bit taken aback by Jesus's boldness in speaking out at such a sacred moment in the ceremony. I was not even aware that he was in attendance. Yet in this most sacred of moments he had purposely drawn the attention of the entire crowd toward himself rather than to the ceremony itself. Suddenly, it dawned on me. The whole ceremony was designed to point to him! The joy was not to be in the pouring of the water from Siloam but in the living water of the Spirit, which Jesus came to give to all who would receive him.

Like a shaft of light pierces through the skies of a cloudy day, this truth brought light to my mind, and the whole ceremony of the Feast of Tabernacles made sense to me. God was sending his Son to us to give each of us that which would quench the thirsting of our souls.

I had felt the living water of which Jesus spoke. The Spirit filled my soul with joy and gladness and made alive in me all the godly desires of my heart. It brought to my mind the feelings I had experienced when I had first kissed Jesus as a babe in Bethlehem. I had wanted to do and become everything that was good and right in life. I had tried by myself to become that goodness, but I had failed time and time again. In coming to Jesus, I felt those seeds of godliness watered and nourished so that they could grow in me to make of me all the good that I desired to become. It was as if I was the basin into which the water was being poured. I was being filled to the brim with the Spirit of the Lord and his love for me and for all his children, whom I now saw as my brothers and sisters. I began to weep for the joy I now felt and the understanding that filled my heart and mind. Truly, this was a feast to give thanks for the Savior, whom God had given to fill our souls with joy.

Chapter 11

Power amid Persecution

As we returned that day to the home of my in-laws, they were more than a bit troubled. "How could he speak up right in the middle of one of the most sacred ceremonies of the feast?" they asked. "He did not appear as the humble carpenter of which you have spoken. If he were truly the Son of God, would he not have had respect for what we do to worship God?"

As we were attempting to explain the symbolism of what Jesus had done, the pharisaic friends of our in-laws came to the door. They were incensed at the audacity of Jesus to make a mockery of such a holy and sacred moment. They had come knowing our belief in Jesus, and they hoped to dissuade us from our convictions. As they railed on Jesus regarding his arrogance to interrupt such a sacred ceremony, I could see the shadow of doubt begin to darken the light that had filled the countenance of my in-laws just days before. Truly, this was a great trial to their newfound faith. I could tell that they wanted to believe, but the persuasion and reasoning of their friends caused them great concern and doubt.

With a courage I had never before felt in my life, I spoke boldly and resolutely to these learned men. My words came clearly and convincingly from a source I did not know I possessed. As I spoke, my heart became even more certain of the things I heard flowing from my lips. I told them of the joy that I had felt in the presence of Jesus and the light that filled my mind each time I heard him speak. I testified boldly that he was indeed the only begotten Son of God, who came to bring light, truth, and living water to those who came with humble and receptive hearts.

Then with a boldness and clarity that surprised even me, my wife spoke of the healing and change that she had felt from a mere touch of the Savior's robe. She testified that Jesus was the Messiah and had come to fulfill the law of Moses, which was insufficient to bring healing and salvation to the people. She told how she had tried every way under the law to find healing for her illness, but only through Jesus had the miracle come. As she spoke, light radiated from her countenance, and she stood before these learned men as a lion among lambs.

Unaffected by the spirit of such a powerful witness, these learned men of the law became incensed that a woman would speak so boldly in their presence. They began to revile and rebuke her, but my father-in-law stepped forward and bid them cease such slander against his daughter. It was apparent that he had been moved by her words and was reassured in his fledgling faith. His wife joined him by his side and politely but firmly asked the men to leave. The men became indignant and assured my in-laws that they could consider themselves unwelcome in the synagogue and no longer of any social standing. One of the men spat upon the ground as they departed, issuing an oath of disdain and derision upon their household.

We stood in silence for several moments after their departure. I could tell that my in-laws were reflecting upon what this would mean for them and their future. They had just given up their old lives for a man whom they did not know for themselves but in whom they had believed through our witness. I marveled at their courage despite the newness of their faith. It was apparent that their love for their daughter and belief in her words had allowed them to hearken to the Spirit of the Lord and had given them the courage to withstand the persecution of their friends.

My wife and I reached out to embrace and reassure them that they had chosen the better part and that their current concerns would be replaced by a sure witness of the divinity of Jesus. I felt sure that such a sacrifice would surely be seen by the Savior in secret and rewarded openly by our Father in heaven. I longed to remove the worry from their heart, but I knew this was a peace that only a sure witness of the Savior would bring.

Chapter 12

Stones of Blindness

The next morning, we went early to the temple with my in-laws to offer our morning sacrifices. To my great joy, Jesus was at the temple, teaching a small crowd that had gathered around to hear his words. I had hoped for an opportunity to introduce my in-laws to the Savior, so we led them up as close as we could through the crowd. We joined the group and felt the power of Jesus's words fill our hearts with understanding and joy. I could tell that my in-laws were very moved and felt the truth of Jesus's message. Being near the Savior allowed them to feel the power of his presence and his great love for all.

As Jesus was concluding his teachings, several of the Scribes and the Pharisees walked through our group to confront him. They had brought with them a woman whom they claimed they had taken in the very act of adultery. They spoke to Jesus, reminding him of the penalty of stoning required by the law of Moses, and then asked what he would have them do to the woman.

As if he didn't hear them, Jesus turned, stooped to the ground, and began writing with his finger in the sand. I strained to see what he was writing, but I was unable to make out the words. The men seemed indignant and continued to insist that Jesus respond. Finally, he stood and said, "He that is without sin among you, let him first cast a stone at her."[43] Jesus again returned to his writing in the sand.

Slowly, one by one, the men who had brought the woman began to leave. When they had all departed, Jesus looked up to find the woman weeping. He asked her gently, "Woman, where are those thine accusers? Hath no man condemned thee?"

She replied incredulously, "No man, Lord."

And Jesus said unto her, "Neither do I condemn thee: go, and sin no more."[44] Joy seemed to fill her countenance. She knelt before the Savior, and with broken sobs, she promised to repent and change her life. I smiled. I knew her gratitude. I had felt that same loving-kindness and mercy from the Lord, and I knew what was beginning in her heart.

As she departed, I led my in-laws forward to meet Jesus. When he turned and saw me, he immediately embraced me. I was almost overcome with emotion as I returned his embrace. I could have remained in that embrace forever. It seemed to be love in its purest form, and it filled every fiber of my being with joy and light.

As we separated, he saw my wife and took her into his arms. I was amazed at how much joy I felt as he embraced her. I felt even more united with the Savior as I felt his love for her. It was as if his love was now allowing me to feel love toward others and seek for all to know and embrace Jesus as their Savior.

Following their embrace, my wife turned and joyfully brought her parents to meet Jesus. He placed his hands upon their shoulders, drew them close, and then looked deeply into their eyes. "You have given much to come," he said. They looked at each other in questioning disbelief. It was as if Jesus knew their thoughts and felt all that they had experienced. He lovingly assured them, "He that loseth his life for my sake, shall find it."[45]

The gentleness of his tone, the love in his eyes, and the assurance of his words touched their hearts. I could see the uncertainty of the previous evening leaving their countenance and being replaced by faith, hope, and love. They reached out and grasped Jesus's arm, returning his gaze and whispering words of gratitude. They assured Jesus that they would be forever grateful for what he had done for their daughter and for them. "We would be honored if you would sup with us," they said. Jesus thanked them for their kindness and agreed to join us for our evening meal.

As we began walking toward the home of my in-laws, we paused to observe as the large candelabras were being removed from the square. Several people had stopped to marvel at the size and magnificence of the lights that lit the city during the feast. Jesus then spoke aloud to the people in the square, "I am the light of the world: he that followeth me shall not walk in darkness, but shall have the light of life."[46]

His words caught the attention of several Pharisees who were overseeing the removal of the lights. They immediately turned on Jesus and said, "Thou bearest record of thyself; thy record is not true."

Jesus answered and said unto them, "Though I bear record of myself, yet my record is true: for I know whence I came, and whither I go; but ye cannot tell whence I come, and whither I go. I am one that bear witness of myself, and the Father that sent me beareth witness of me."

The Pharisees then inquired, "Where is thy Father?"

Jesus answered, "Ye neither know me, nor my Father: if ye had known me, ye should have known my Father also."[47]

Then Jesus turned directly to those who were questioning him and said, "When ye have lifted up the Son of man, then shall ye know that I am he, and that I do nothing of myself; but as my Father hath taught me, I speak these things. And he that sent me is with me: the Father hath not left me alone; for I do always those things that please him."[48]

The power of Jesus's words left me with a confirmation of their truth that was undeniable. Several of those around me felt the same Spirit. Jesus then turned from those who were accusing him to face us and said, "If ye continue in my word, then are ye my disciples indeed; And ye shall know the truth, and the truth shall make you free."[49]

These words incensed the Pharisees, who retorted, "We be Abraham's seed, and were never in bondage to any man: how sayest thou, Ye shall be made free?"[50] I almost choked at their words. Never been in bondage? Did they not remember the history of their ancestors, who had known little but bondage since the days when Israel was ruled by the pharaohs? They themselves were now in bondage to the Romans! Could they not see their need for freedom?

Jesus answered them, "Verily, verily, I say unto you, Whosoever committeth sin is the servant of sin. And the servant abideth not in the house for ever: but the Son abideth ever. If the Son therefore shall make you free, ye shall be free indeed."[51]

Freedom. That is what I felt when I was with Jesus. Freedom from my sin, my doubt, my self-concern, my worry, and my fear. I was free to feel his love for me and for those around me. Why was it that these men could not understand and feel this for themselves? Were they so hardened, arrogant, and self-assured that they could not feel the power of the Savior's words?

The Pharisees continued to argue with Jesus, but he answered them boldly without anger or contention but with a firmness that assured all of us around him that what he spoke was the truth.

One of the Pharisees, speaking for the group, said unto Jesus, "Abraham is our father."

Jesus replied, "If ye were Abraham's children, ye would do the works of Abraham. But now ye seek to kill me, a man that hath told you the truth, which I have heard of God: this did not Abraham. Ye do the deeds of your father."

Indignant at his insinuation, the Pharisees replied, "We be not born of fornication; we have one Father, even God."

Jesus said unto them, "If God were your Father, ye would love me: for I proceeded forth and came from God; neither came I of myself, but he sent me. Why do ye not understand my speech? even because ye cannot hear my word. Ye are of your father the devil, and the lusts of your father ye will do. He was a murderer from the beginning, and abode not in the truth, because there is no truth in him. When he speaketh a lie, he speaketh of his own: for he is a liar, and the father of it. And because I tell you the truth, ye believe me not."[52]

We all stood a bit stunned. Had Jesus just told the most prominent leaders among the Jews that they were children of the devil? Irate beyond anything I had seen before among this class, which usually held themselves aloof from even talking to the common people, they angrily sought to discredit Jesus and said, “Say we not well that thou art a Samaritan, and hast a devil?”

Jesus answered boldly, “I have not a devil; but I honor my Father, and ye do dishonor me. Verily, verily, I say unto you, If a man keep my saying, he shall never see death.”

Then said the Jews unto him, “Now we know that thou hast a devil. Abraham is dead, and the prophets; and thou sayest, If a man keep my saying, he shall never taste of death. Art thou greater than our father Abraham, which is dead? and the prophets are dead: whom makest thou thyself?”

Jesus answered, “If I honor myself, my honor is nothing: it is my Father that honoreth me; of whom ye say, that he is your God: Yet ye have not known him; but I know him: and if I should say, I know him not, I shall be a liar like unto you: but I know him, and keep his saying. Your father Abraham rejoiced to see my day: and he saw it, and was glad.”

Then said the Jews unto him, “Thou art not yet fifty years old, and hast thou seen Abraham?”

Jesus said unto them, “Verily, verily, I say unto you, Before Abraham was, I AM.”[53]

Had my ears deceived me? In declaring, “Before Abraham was, I AM,” Jesus was declaring himself to be Jehovah, the God of our Fathers! Jesus stood with a certain resolve and confident air that left no doubt that he stood firm in his declaration. As I pondered on his words, the Spirit filled my soul with confirmation as to Jesus’s place and position before coming to earth. Truly, Jesus was in very deed the God of our fathers and the Son of God the eternal Father.

The cry of blaspheme hissed forth from the lips of every Pharisee and Scribe who had heard Jesus speak. They took up stones to cast at him just as they had intended to inflict death upon the adulterous woman. Filled with venomous hatred toward Jesus, however, there was no hesitation this time in their conscience as to their own sins. Certain that Jesus was worthy of death, they stood prepared to be both judges and executioners.

I feared for Jesus's life, but then something miraculous occurred. Jesus went out of the temple, going through the midst of them as if he was hidden from their view. I marveled that they simply let him pass by. Blinded by their hatred and rage, they were unable to see not only who he was but also his physical presence. He truly was the light—a light that could only be seen by those who believed in him and acknowledged his divinity. Jesus was a God who is unseen to the sceptic but is ever-present to the pure in heart and to those who see with the eye of faith.

Chapter 13

Seeing and Sinning

Our evening meal was truly a feast, not only for the sumptuous fare provided by my in-laws but also for the spiritual nourishment provided us by the Savior while we ate. I had heard Jesus preach many times in the past year, but this reminded me of the intimate time I had spent with him when he was just a boy teaching me by the temple. Feasting upon the Word of God in the quiet intimacy of a home filled with the Savior's presence filled my heart with great peace and joy.

I asked Jesus if he would be returning to Galilee in the morning. He replied that he would remain and teach in and around Jerusalem until his time had come. Then he would return to Jerusalem to become the Passover. I turned to my wife with a curious glance. She returned mine with a questioning look of her own. Did he just say, "To become the Passover?" Surely, he meant to say, "To attend the Passover." I smilingly said, "Don't you mean that you will attend the Passover?"

He returned my inquiry with a solemn gaze and a response that sent a slight chill down my spine. "Remember the day in which ye provided unto my family a lamb for our Passover?" I nodded. "So now must I provide unto you a lamb which shall be slain, that the angel of death might pass over you and your household, that ye might be saved. The Son of man is delivered into the hands of men, and they shall kill him; and after that he is killed, he shall rise the third day."[54]

We all looked at each other, wondering at his words but afraid to inquire further. He bid us good evening and returned to be with his other disciples. We retired for the evening, but sleep fled as my mind raced, pondering the words of Jesus. I had planned to return to Galilee to get back to the business of my shop, but I felt the need to remain with Jesus and seek to understand the words he had spoken. I felt certain that this was to be a Passover like no other, and I desired to be with him even if it meant giving up all that I possessed.

In the morning I spoke to my father-in-law. He had had similar impressions. We decided that we would sell the shop in Galilee and my wife and I would move in with them. In return, I would help maintain the shop here in Jerusalem. This would allow us to be close to Jesus and hear him preach.

This day being the Sabbath, we made our way to the synagogue to worship. Despite the threats of their Pharisaical friends from a few nights previous, we intended to attend as God commanded. As we neared the pool at Siloam, we saw a man washing his face in the waters of the pool, the very waters from which the priests had drawn the water for the ceremony of the Feast of Tabernacles. As he came up from the pool, he exclaimed that he could now see. Several people curiously came to see. One of them inquired, "Is not this he that sat and begged?" Some said that it was, but others said, "He is like him."

But he said, "I am he."

They then asked him, "How were thine eyes opened?"

He responded, "A man that is called Jesus made clay, and anointed my eyes, and said unto me, Go to the pool of Siloam, and wash: and I went and washed, and I received sight."[55]

Hearing the man testify that Jesus had given him his sight instilled in me a greater understanding of Jesus's teaching the previous day that he is the light of the world. He was more than an example to follow. He was indeed the very light by which we could see God and wash away the blindness brought on by focusing on the things of this world. Surely, if Jesus could heal a man who had been blind from his birth, he could open the spiritual eyes of those who had been blinded by the things of the world—that is, if they were willing to come unto him and be born again.

As we proceeded to synagogue, I marveled at the many disputations taking place as to Jesus's power. The Pharisees were proclaiming Jesus to be a sinner because he had done that which was not lawful on the Sabbath. Hearing them argue such things made me wonder if they had not lost sight of the purpose of the Sabbath. Was this not a day to delight ourselves in the Lord by caring for the poor, as Isaiah had said?[56] Surely, one could not do more to honor the Sabbath than by helping others in need of assistance. A Sabbath spent in living the gospel—serving the Lord and others—must surely be as uplifting and enlightening as a day spent in attending the synagogue. Does not one learn more in the doing than in the hearing? True one must be taught how to live, but in the end, it is not the learning of such things but the doing of them that lifts us up.

We left off our intention to attend the synagogue and sought instead to be instructed by Jesus. We found him talking to the man whom he had healed. He quietly asked him, "Dost thou believe in the Son of God?"

The man replied, "Who is he, Lord, that I might believe on him?"

Jesus responded, "Thou hast both seen him, and it is he that talketh with thee." At this the man fell at the Savior's feet, worshipping him. Jesus gently raised him to his feet, embraced him, and said, "For judgment I am come in to the world, that they which see not might see; and that they which see might be made blind."[57]

Some of the priests who were standing near enough to hear Jesus's remarks became infuriated. They asked cynically, "Are we blind also?"

Jesus turned and said, "If ye were blind, ye should have no sin, but now ye say, 'We see;' therefore your sin remaineth."[58]

Again, Jesus's words penetrated my heart as with shafts of light that chased any darkness of doubt from my mind. He is the light. If we see by that light but still refuse to follow and live according to that light, then we are held accountable. Once enlightened, we can no longer live below the light we have received. If we know to do good and don't do it, then we are in sin. Sin is not just those things we do that are not right. It is also those things we know to be right but do not do. If we know that we should stop and help another in need and do not do so, we have sinned against the light we possess.

I began to wonder if it would be better to simply live in ignorance rather than seek more light which, if I chose not to obey, would only bring condemnation. As a voice from within, the Spirit whispered that only by living according to greater light could I experience the joy that comes from such living. God does not give us more knowledge to make us miserable but to give us the opportunity to live life as he lives it. Being able to live all that God teaches me takes time to practice and requires repeated repentance, yet I have felt the joy that comes when I am able to follow his teachings, which motivates me to seek more diligently to do as he directs.

The Pharisees indeed realized the good things Jesus was doing for the people, but they also recognized that he was elevating the common man, which caused them to lose their power and station. Their pride would not allow them to humbly acknowledge the truth of his sayings, and so they remained as ones who loved the darkness more than the light. As Isaiah had warned, they gloried in their own self-righteousness and walked in the light of their own fire and in the sparks that they themselves had kindled.[59] They did not seek to come unto God according to the Way, the Truth, and the Light, which he had sent.

Chapter 14

The Good Shepherd

I found myself enthralled by every word Jesus spoke. I felt as if my soul was being taught directly from heaven. It was as if his teachings were things I had once known down deep in my soul but had merely forgotten. I wondered why the learned men of the Pharisees could not feel and understand what was ringing so profoundly true in my heart.

Jesus looked at me and smiled as if he were reading my thoughts. Then using a parable to explain the reason for their lack of understanding, Jesus said, "He that entereth in by the door is the shepherd of the sheep. To him the porter openeth; and the sheep hear his voice: and he calleth his own sheep by name, and leadeth them out. And when he putteth forth his own sheep, he goeth before them, and the sheep follow him: for they know his voice. And a stranger will they not follow, but will flee from him: for they know not the voice of strangers."[60]

Having spent a good part of my life as a shepherd, I understood exactly what Jesus was saying. I knew each of my sheep personally, and they knew me. When I came to the sheepfold each morning, I would call each of them by name. They were familiar with my voice and would come out from among the other sheep who ignored me and waited for the voice of their own masters.

Obviously, the Pharisees did not recognize the voice of Jesus as their master and the one they were to follow. I was certain that they did not understand this parable as they began to question among themselves the meaning of his sayings. I realized why Jesus had spoken so frequently in parables. They were masterfully crafted about daily things the common people would hear and understand, but they would completely confound the hearts and minds of those who were not ready to follow his teachings.

Then said Jesus unto them again, "Verily, verily, I say unto you, I am the door of the sheep: by me if any man enter in, he shall be saved, and shall go in and out, and find pasture. The thief cometh not, but for to steal, and to kill, and to destroy: I am come that they might have life, and that they might have it more abundantly.

"I am the good shepherd: the good shepherd giveth his life for the sheep. But he that is an hireling, and not the shepherd, whose own the sheep are not, seeth the wolf coming, and leaveth the sheep, and fleeth: and the wolf catcheth them, and scattereth the sheep."

"I am the good shepherd, and know my sheep, and am known of mine. As the Father knoweth me, even so know I the Father: and I lay down my life for the sheep. And other sheep I have, which are not of this fold: them also I must bring, and they shall hear my voice; and there shall be one fold, and one shepherd."

"Therefore doth my Father love me, because I lay down my life, that I might take it again. No man taketh it from me, but I lay it down of myself. I have power to lay it down, and I have power to take it again. This commandment have I received of my Father."[61]

Jesus's words struck the chords of truth within my heart. They were as music from heaven but with a melancholy melody. I knew the love of a shepherd in being willing to give his life for the sheep, yet he had said that he was to be the Lamb of the Passover. Was he to be both shepherd and sacrificial lamb? I could feel in my heart the love of the Savior in speaking such tender words, but my mind was still uncertain how he was to both protect us as a shepherd while being the lamb that would be slain.

After Jesus had spoken these words, there was again a division among the Jews. Many of them said, "He hath a devil, and is mad;

why hear ye him?" Others said, "These are not the words of him that hath a devil. Can a devil open the eyes of the blind?"[62]

Quickly, several of the Jews came round about him and said unto him, "How long dost thou make us to doubt? If thou be the Christ, tell us plainly."

With a voice that was both clear and calm, Jesus answered them, "I told you, and ye believed not: the works that I do in my Father's name, they bear witness of me. But ye believe not, because ye are not of my sheep, as I said unto you. My sheep hear my voice, and I know them, and they follow me: and I give unto them eternal life; and they shall never perish, neither shall any man pluck them out of my hand. My Father, which gave them me, is greater than all; and no man is able to pluck them out of my Father's hand. I and my Father are one."[63]

Once again, the Jewish leaders took up stones to stone him, and Jesus asked them simply, "Many good works have I shown you from my Father; for which of those works do ye stone me?"

The Jews answered him, "For a good work we stone thee not; but for blasphemy; and because that thou, being a man, makest thyself God."

Jesus answered them, "Is it not written in your law, I said, Ye are gods? If he called them gods, unto whom the word of God came, and the scripture cannot be broken; Say ye of him, whom the Father hath sanctified, and sent into the world, Thou blasphemest; because I said, I am the Son of God? If I do not the works of my Father, believe me not. But if I do, though ye believe not me, believe the works: that ye may know, and believe, that the Father is in me, and I in him."[64]

Incensed at Jesus's declaration that he and the Father were one, the Pharisees sought to take him, but he escaped out of their hands. I again marveled at their inability to take him. It seemed no man could take him unless he allowed it to be so. This left me to wonder at things yet to be.

Chapter 15

What Lack I Yet?

The ensuing days were busy indeed. Reluctant to leave Jerusalem, my wife and I nevertheless made our way back to Capernaum to sell the shop, our home, and our personal belongings before making our way back to Jerusalem for the Passover. Providence smiled upon our journey, and we were able to dispense with all in a very short time. Some thought that we sacrificed too much, yet we felt no attachment to our worldly goods. We sought only to be with the Lord in Jerusalem for the Passover.

As we made our return journey, we passed through the land of Perea, where the Lord had been teaching since the days of the Feast of Tabernacle. Many people had flocked to hear him teach, and all seemed to be clamoring for his association and recognition. Even among the Twelve, there was discussion about who was greatest among the followers. I smiled within as I recalled my earlier concerns about my station and position among his followers. It seemed so unimportant now—who served in what position or calling. From the greatest to the least, all were alike unto Jesus.

We noticed how the little children were especially drawn to the Savior. Unconcerned about calling or station, they only desired the light of his love and the joy of his embrace. On one occasion, the disciples rebuked those who brought the children unto Jesus. This displeased the Savior, and with the kindness and tenderness of a father, he beckoned them to bring the children unto him. I could not help but smile as I saw him embrace, tickle, and laugh with the children. Taking each one into his arms, he blessed them and prayed for them and then taught all of us that we needed to be like those children if we were to enter into the kingdom of God.

In my mind's eye, I could see my return to my Father's presence. I did not come with personal belongings, but with the innocence and joy of a child coming to meet his daddy. I could see the light in his face and the joy in his countenance. I felt myself encircled within his loving arms and clasped to his bosom as his child joyfully returning home after a long journey. The vision in my mind seemed so real that I could feel his love warm me to my very center. My wife touched my arm, and I was brought abruptly back to our place on the hillside, watching Jesus with the children.

As Jesus placed the last of the children back into the arms of her smiling parents, he saw us standing a short distance from him and stood to make his way toward us. As he did so, a man fell at his feet and asked, "Good Master, what shall I do that I may inherit eternal life?"

The man was well dressed, and by the jewels he wore, he appeared to be a man of great means. Jesus's answer surprised many. "Why callest thou me good? None is good, save one. That is God."[65] If ever I had known someone good, it was Jesus. I marveled at how he continued to deflect all honor and praise to his Father.

Turning to the man, he then said, "Thou knowest the commandments. Do not commit adultery. Do not kill. Do not steal. Do not bear false witness. Honor thy father and mother."

The man then answered, "All these have I kept from my youth up."

As Jesus gazed upon him, I could see in the Savior's eyes a great love for this man. He looked up to see us standing there and then said to the man, "Yet lackest thou one thing: sell all that thou hast, and distribute to the poor, and thou shalt have treasure in heaven: and come, follow me."[66] Startled, the man looked up at the Savior, who had now fastened his gaze down upon him. I sensed a sadness in his eyes as he returned the Savior's gaze. He stood and went away, grieved because he had great possessions.

Jesus seemed saddened at the man's response and turned toward his disciples and said, "How hardly shall they that have riches enter into the kingdom of God?"[67] I could tell that this saying troubled many of his listeners. Then as if to remind them of what they had just experienced in seeing him with the little ones, Jesus said, "Children, how hard is it for them that trust in riches to enter into the kingdom of God!"[68]

Jesus had just told us all that in order to enter into the kingdom of God, we had to become as little children. Children do not concern themselves with many things or how many possessions they have. They find joy in playing with a simple stick or with their family and friends. They do not concern themselves with the size of their home or number of coins in their pockets.

The reaction of this good brother, who had sincerely come unto Jesus with a desire to follow him, told me that he had allowed his possessions to possess his heart and keep him from coming to God as a little child. Somehow in gaining possessions of the world, many see themselves as "grown up" and masters of their own world, forgetting that it is God who has provided all for us and that truly all belongs to him. When we give our hearts to God, we cannot therefore set our hearts on riches.

I began to wonder why Jesus had not asked me to sell everything I had and give it to the poor. I still had the coins in my bag from the profit we had made in selling our goods. This he must have known. Was this his way of asking us to give away all that we had earned from the sale of our home and goods? I would readily give all to him if he had asked, but this he must also have known.

As I pondered these things in mind and my heart, I realized that it was not riches that the Savior desires from his followers. It is our hearts. He did not ask me for my riches because he knew that I would readily give them to him. He had asked of me that which had taken possession of my heart and had prevented me from giving my all to God—my doubts, self-centeredness, and fear.

In one small moment of startling clarity, Jesus had opened my mind to what truly mattered in life. It became clear to me why we had felt moved to leave our possessions in Capernaum. Our hearts longed to be with him regardless of what was asked. As I pondered these things, Jesus stepped forward and gently touched my arm, stirring me from my internal whisperings. I smiled at his face, and my wife and I embraced him. "Go unto Jerusalem," he said gently, "for I shall have need of thee and thy Father's house at the time of the feast. I will send unto you Peter and John, and they shall help you in your preparations."

My wife and I looked at each other and then smiled at Jesus and assured him that we would make all ready for him. He touched our shoulders, smiled upon us, and thanked us as he bid us farewell. We felt his love, trust, and gratitude as we journeyed back to the home of my wife's parents.

Chapter 16

Entrance of the King

Jerusalem, which had always been a center of life and activity during the Passover, seemed especially full of excitement and anticipation when we returned to the house of my in-laws. They had prepared their guesthouse for us upon our return. They were very happy to see us, but I could see some concern in their eyes about the coming events. They had heard that some of their former friends were planning to publicly humiliate Jesus if he dared come to Jerusalem for the feast. We assured them that Jesus knew what was ahead and would come prepared and ready to meet whatever challenge could be thrust upon him. We told him of Jesus's words to us to prepare our home as he would have need of us for the feast. This seemed to change their concerns into pure joy over the thought of sharing the Passover with the Messiah.

I spent the next few days organizing the shop of my father-in-law to accommodate the merchandise from our old shop in Capernaum. I worked closely with Cleopus, one of my father-in-law's best workers and a recent convert to the teachings of Jesus. He told me about how my father-in-law had told him about the Messiah and what he had done for his daughter. His heart had been touched, and he believed all that he had been taught.

Cleopus was eager to work with me, as he had heard about how I had known Jesus since his birth. He had a multitude of questions, and we talked about many of my experiences while we organized the displays of material for sale.

While working one day, I caught sight of a man stopping to look at some of the textiles. I knew him immediately. "Luke!" I almost shouted. He looked up from the cloth he was examining and looked into my face. With a shout of joy and exaltation, he grabbed me and pulled me to his bosom. We embraced for several moments before I asked him, "What, my good friend, are you doing in Jerusalem? Come to buy some of the finest cotton in all the land?" Holding up some of the cloth he had been examining, I smiled broadly and winked.

"Much more than that, my friend," he replied. "Since our encounter upon the road to Jericho, I have set my life to helping people as you helped me. I am now a physician so that I might tend to the needs of others. But I have discovered something even more healing than the craft I have learned. Do you remember Jesus of whom you spoke when you helped me along the roadside?"

"Remember him?" I replied. "I have spent the last three years following and serving with him. I have become one of his disciples. My wife and I recently moved here to be closer to Jesus. He is coming to spend the Passover feast with us at the home of my wife's parents. Luke, I have come to know that he is the true Messiah of Israel."

Luke smiled broadly at me. "I have also come to Jerusalem to meet Jesus. The Spirit has witnessed to me that he is not only the Messiah of the Jews, but I believe that he is the very Son of God come to show all men the way to heaven. I have heard much of his teachings while in my homeland of Greece. I have come to write his story so that I might share it with my friends back home who have also heard the stories of the miracles Jesus has wrought. Is it true that he walked on the water and the very seas obey his commands?"

"It is true, my friend! I was there upon the boat when he came to us in the night. I have seen with my own eyes many of the miracles of which you speak. But the greatest of all his miracles that I have witnessed is the healing of the souls of men. He has healed mine. I have come to know the miracle of his love and his divine power to change hearts and bring all to the light of God. He is indeed God's own Son, and he has come to save us!"

I saw in Luke's face a joy and light that I had seen in others who have come to recognize Jesus as the Son of God. He asked if I would be willing to share with him some of the things I had seen, heard, and learned in my journeys with Jesus. I assured him that I would be honored to recount to him all that I remembered. We walked to a nearby cafe and shared a meal as I recounted to him the things I had experienced. They had left an indelible mark upon my soul, and more than anything, I wanted to share with others what I had learned and come to know by following Jesus.

The sun began to drop lower and lower in the sky as we visited through the afternoon. Luke scribbled wildly as we talked, drinking in every word as if they were the waters of life. Indeed, they were the very waters Jesus had promised the woman at the well who had first brought me word that Jesus had come. I could feel the Spirit of the Lord guide my thoughts and recollections as I unfolded what to me was the greatest story ever told. As I reflected on all that I had experienced with Jesus and the change that had come to my life, I prayed that Luke would be able to capture that same spirit in the words he would write so that the power of his words might touch the hearts of others and change their lives as mine had been changed.

As evening approached, I invited Luke to come and spend the night with us at the home of my in-laws. I wanted him to meet my sweet wife and her family who had given up so much to follow Jesus. He thanked me, but he said he had to go to be with his family, which was awaiting his return at the nearby inn where he and his wife had secured lodging during their time in Jerusalem. He assured me that he would stop by the store again before he departed. We embraced, and then he departed toward the inn. I could not help but smile as I watched him go.

The ensuing days were filled with an intensity I had seldom seen in my lifetime. Word spread throughout the city that Jesus had raised one of his friends from the dead. I heard it noised around the marketplace that the Sanhedrin had counseled together and had sworn to put Jesus to death. Knowing my parents' growing connection with Jesus, their Pharisaical friends came by their home and warned them that if they saw or heard from Jesus, they were to inform the group immediately so that they might take him to prevent him from disrupting the sacredness and holiness of the Passover as he had done at the Feast of Tabernacles. They warned each of us that if they found us helping him, we would face severe punishment from the council.

Despite all the threats and tension, there seemed also to be a swelling feeling of hope among the people that the true Messiah had finally come to his people. Several days before the feast, I heard that Jesus had spent the day in Bethany, sharing a meal with Lazarus, his friend whom he had restored to life. One of my friends told me that he had heard the chief priests conspiring to have Lazarus put to death to stop the people from believing that Jesus was a God who had power over death itself.

Just a few days before the feast, we received word that Jesus would be entering the city the next morning from the Mount of Olives. My wife, her parents, and I went early in the morning to the place where the road from the Mount of Olives entered the city. As I came upon the place where the crowd had gathered, the excitement of the scene reminded me of how I felt when I was a boy in the fields of Bethlehem and the angel proclaimed the coming of the Savior to the earth. I could hardly believe that I was now witnessing his triumphal entry into Jerusalem to take his place as Lord and King over the people of Israel.

As I stood near the gate into the city, I saw Jesus coming down the side of the Mount of Olives. A huge throng of people had now gathered to welcome him into the city. His disciples provided a small donkey for him to ride as he entered through the gate. Many of us cut down palm leaves and waved them in the air as a sign of royal welcome. Others placed the palm leaves upon the ground and carpeted the way for him to pass. Robes and outer clothing were stripped and laid before him.

I caught my wife's gaze as we saw him come. The moment was too glorious for words. Here at last, Jesus was finally being acknowledged as the King and deliverer of Israel. We all joined in shouting, "Hosanna to the Son of David: Blessed is he that cometh in the name of the Lord; Hosanna in the highest! Blessed be the King that cometh in the name of the Lord: peace in heaven, and glory in the highest."[69] Surely Jesus, the Son of King David, who had freed Israel from so many other Gentile nations, had come to save us now and end our many years of suffering and bondage to the power of Rome.

My mind was again drawn to the time when, as a boy, I heard the great multitude of angels sing on that glorious night, "Glory to God in the highest, and on earth, peace to men of good will!"[70] I desired to lift my voice as with the angels and proclaim to the whole world that this was indeed our Savior and Messiah whom had been prophesied for generations would come. And now he was here! I embraced my wife, and we wept for joy over what we were blessed to witness. Truly, this was the most joyous moment that anyone could hope to experience in a thousand lifetimes.

Some of the Pharisees from among the multitude shouted at Jesus, "Master, rebuke thy disciples."

But gazing upon the people, Jesus simply smiled and answered, "I tell you that, if these should hold their peace, the stones would immediately cry out."[71]

I could see in their faces that they were infuriated at his reply and desired to take him immediately before the high priest and have him sanctioned and denounced. However, the multitude thronged Jesus and continued to proclaim him as their king. Fearing what the people might do, the Pharisees departed, but I sensed that they were not finished in their attempts to take him. For a moment,

I feared that they would seek him in a private moment when he would not have the support of the people. But nothing could diminish the joy of this moment of Jesus's triumphant entry into the city. Truly, Israel was about to be saved by their one true King.

Chapter 17

First Cleanse the Inner Vessel

Shortly after his entrance into the city, to the surprise of many, Jesus did not make his way to the palace of Pilate, the military leader of the Roman brigade that kept Jerusalem under strict Roman rule. Instead we followed him as he made his way to the temple. Upon entering, Jesus became more upset than I had witnessed in all my travels with him. With an intensity that brought fear to those trading and exchanging money at the tables, he overthrew the tables and cast all of them from the temple. Incensed at their indifference to and desecration of the sacredness of the house of God, Jesus spoke with authority and power, "My house is the house of prayer; but ye have made it a den of thieves."[72] Angered by his actions, the money changers ran to complain to the Pharisees about what Jesus had done.

As the chief priests arrived at the temple, they found Jesus healing all who would come to him. We marveled as the blind received their sight and the lame walked. All who came were healed by Jesus. We rejoiced that all could now see that he had indeed come from heaven to heal the people. Everyone cried and proclaimed aloud that he was the chosen Messiah who had come to save Israel.

Displeased at their shouts of praise and adoration, the chief priests approached Jesus to have him silence the crowd. With a smile that must have truly angered them, he asked, "Have ye never read, Out of the mouth of babes and sucklings thou has perfected praise."[73]

During the next few days preceding the feast, Jesus taught daily in the temple words of life and the good news of God's deliverance for the people. My wife and I sat at his feet and marveled at his wisdom and understanding of the scriptures. His words illuminated our minds with light and truth. In all our previous time with the Savior, we had not heard him teach with such power and directness. I wondered how anyone could hear the truths he taught and not feel their power in their hearts.

While the multitudes continued to throng Jesus in order to hear his teachings, the Scribes and Pharisees made repeated efforts to challenge him. Oftentimes Jesus would respond with parables that left them without response. When they challenged his authority to teach, he responded by asking them a question about the authority of John the Baptist, whether it was from God or from man. Knowing how the crowd revered John as a prophet sent from God yet having not followed him themselves, they declined to answer his question. Knowing the hardness of their hearts, Jesus refused to tell them the source of his authority. Again, I marveled. How could any man hear him and not feel the power of the Spirit as he spoke, witnessing that he had indeed come from God.

As the week progressed, the Scribes and Pharisees became more aggressive in their efforts to discredit Jesus in front of the multitude in order to turn them against him. Jesus answered each affront with penetrating parables that pointed back to those of the Sanhedrin, convicting them of their hypocrisy and heresy toward God. When Jesus told the parables of the wicked husbandmen and the marriage of the son of the king, there was no mistaking the Savior's intent to show the Sanhedrin who they truly were--servants who had been called but had usurped authority and ignored God's will to help and bless the people.

Toward the end of the week, the Sanhedrin tried desperately to twist Jesus's words to give them cause to have him taken before Rome for treason. Jesus perceived their evil intent and taught that all men should render unto Caesar the things that belong to Caesar but render to God those things that belong to God.[74] Each response from Jesus resonated with truth that infuriated the Scribes, Pharisees, and Sadducees, and they were left without answer for Jesus or his teachings.

Empowered by their inability to respond to him, the Savior spoke openly to the multitude and his disciples, denouncing the Jewish leaders as hypocrites, blind guides, and fools. He compared them to whited sepulchers who appeared beautiful on the outside but were filled with decay and uncleanness on the inside.[75] Never had I heard Jesus, who repeatedly taught love, tolerance, and kindness, teach with such harshness and judgment, leaving those convicted without excuse or recourse.

During his blistering rebuke of these leaders, I sat next to my wife's parents and sensed their discomfort. While they had strong testimonies that Jesus was the Messiah who had been sent from God to break them free from Rome, many of their friends were among those on the Sanhedrin and were now being openly denounced. As we looked upon many of their former friends, we could see the anger and bitterness welling up inside of them. They were obviously offended with no desire to change or acknowledge Jesus as the Messiah.

As we returned home that evening, my wife's parents asked me why Jesus, who had taught the previous day that the greatest commandment was to love God and the second was to love your fellow man, would then turn and teach with such a condemning and accusatory spirit. "He did not speak with much love for those of the Sanhedrin," commented my father-in-law during our evening meal. "If he truly loved them, would he not seek to reclaim them rather than call them a generation of vipers and accuse them of killing and crucifying the prophets as others had done before them?" He continued, "And why would he say that all of the blood of the righteous would come upon them?"

As I looked into his eyes, I could see that he still desired to believe that Jesus was the Messiah, but he was having serious reservations about the harshness of Jesus's words and his seeming intolerance toward these people whom my father-in-law had once called friends, people with whom he had shared many meals. Once drawn to the Savior by his message of love and forgiveness, he was now finding himself under the shadow of doubt as he contemplated the words of Jesus's scathing rebuke of his former friends. He knew that his friends had been hard-hearted in not being willing to listen to Jesus, but he also knew that many of them were basically good people who had raised themselves to positions of distinction by their service in the synagogues.

I could tell that the question of my father-in-law was born out of a genuine desire to continue to believe, not to doubt the things that he had already received by the power of the Spirit. I struggled to find the words to answer his sincere searching. As I reflected on his question, I began to think about the words of doctrine that Jesus had taught during his ministry. They were difficult for those steeped in their ancient traditions to fully understand and accept. Surely, Jesus should be more tolerant and loving to those whom he perceived had gone astray and strive to bring them into the fold of God. How was this scathing denunciation of their behavior an act of love or concern for them as children of God?

I soon realized that I did not know the answer to my father-in-law's question. As doubt attempted to cloud my mind, I remembered the things that I did know. What I knew without doubt or hesitation was that the Jesus I had come to know was filled with love and concern for all of God's children. He was a man of greater love, compassion, and understanding than any I had known. I had felt his divinity for myself, and nothing could change the witness that I had received by the Spirit that he was the Messiah.

As my faith in what I did know welled up inside of me, doubt was pushed from my mind, and I could again think and see clearly. As if by a light from heaven, the words of Proverbs came pouring into my mind. "My son, despise not the chastening of the Lord; neither be weary of his correction: For whom the Lord loveth he correcteth; even as a father the son in whom he delighteth."[76] The words came as water to the thirsty ground. Immediately, my mind was filled with light and understanding.

I put my hand on my father-in-law's shoulder and taught him the words of the Lord from his scriptures. I could see light come into his eyes as he recognized the truth of these words. He could see, as I now also understood, that Jesus's rebuke of the Sanhedrin was an act of love to try to help them to see how their behavior was turning them from the very God they claimed to worship.

God does indeed look on the heart as the Lord spoke to his ancient prophet Samuel.[77] Even if we are going through the motions and doing all the outward observances, it is the effect that these actions are having upon our hearts that is the true measure of our discipleship and determine what we will become. The Sanhedrin had allowed their outward actions to fill them with pride, vanity, and a disdain for sinners against Mosaic laws and oral traditions. In this state or condition, they could not come unto God. Jesus's bold condemnation of their behavior was an attempt to allow them to see how far they had fallen from the truths of God's gospel of redemption so that they would have the chance to change and repent.

As this truth penetrated deeper and deeper into my soul, I pondered the things that I needed to change within myself. I stood in no position to judge the heart of another, but I could begin to see that I had harbored some thoughts and ideas that I needed to change within me. Perhaps that was another purpose of the Savior's rebuke of the Sanhedrin. He desired that all the people of Israel examine themselves so that they might first cleanse the inner vessel.

Chapter 18

Preparations and the Passover

The morning of the Passover dawned crisp and clear with a hint of the passing winter lingering in the air coupled with the warmth and promise of the blossoming spring. I spent the morning working in the shop before going home to help prepare the guest chamber of my wife's parents' home for the upcoming meal. We had yet to hear from Jesus, but we wanted all to be ready when he came to sup at our home with his apostles. The anticipation of sharing this Passover with the Savior was as the promise of a cool drink on a hot summer afternoon.

I was in the upper room of my father-in-law's home when he brought Peter and John up the small stairway to show them the place where they would dine. When I saw them enter, I greeted them warmly. They seemed a bit surprised to see me since they did not know that this was the home of my father-in-law. "If you did not know this to be where I resided, how did you know where to come?" I asked them. "Did Jesus not tell you that you would dine with me and my family?"

Peter replied, "Jesus simply told us that we were to go into the city, and there we would find a man carrying a pitcher of water. We were instructed to follow him and inquire of the good man of the house as to the guest chamber where the Master was to eat the Passover.[78] Upon our inquiry, your father-in-law led us straightway here."

I smiled at the Savior's knowing of each detail yet his desire to ask his disciples to act in faith. He did not inform Peter and John that he had already let us know that he would celebrate the Passover in our home, but rather he invited them to go into the city and trust that he had prepared all.

I could not help but reflect on the foreknowledge of the Savior in so many aspects of my life and the lives of all of God's children. Yet he continues to invite all to act in faith, not showing us beforehand what lies ahead. He leaves all choices to us so that we might exercise our agency, yet he knows the end from the beginning. He knows not just the end of a singular path for each of us but also each possible path we might choose to follow. When we exercise faith in him, we choose a path that leads us to the greatest joy and happiness despite trials and challenges that come along that path. He knows each of us personally and intimately and knows the things that we must learn in order to become more like our Father in heaven.

This insight brought the realization that when we seek counsel from God in prayer, he will direct us in the path that will provide us the growth that we need and the experience that we came into this life to receive not only to return to live with him but to become like him in the process. To be taught the path that he would have us travel, we must first align our will with his will. He will not impose anything upon us. He will honor our agency and give to us according to our desires. Only as we willingly choose to follow him, align our will with his, and act in faith to do what he instructs us are we able to see the path that he has prepared for us that we might learn and find true heavenly joy.

As I shared these thoughts with Peter and John, we all marveled at the Savior's understanding of all things, including the seemingly simple details of our lives. As we finished our preparations for the feast, we smiled and reflected on the wonderful times we had enjoyed with the Savior over the last three years. I felt humbled that I was able to play a part in what was sure to be a feast that would never be forgotten.

When the Savior arrived with his other apostles in the evening, he greeted me and my wife and my in-laws with his usual warmth and love. While Passover is a joyous time for family, there was a certain solemnity about the Savior that was not typical of his manner. He told us that he had some important things that he must share with his apostles at this meal, and he asked that our family serve rather than sit with them during the feast.

I was a bit disappointed to not be invited to sit and eat with the Savior, but my wife quickly thanked the Savior for the opportunity to serve, took my arm, and led us down to the kitchen to bring up the meal for the apostles and the Savior. Seeing the sheer joy of my wife in being asked to serve the Savior reminded me that to serve others is one of the greatest expressions of love that we can give. I soon joined in the spirit of this labor of love, and we happily provided each course of the sumptuous feast of the Passover meal.

As I passed in and out of the room where they dined, I was able to catch bits and pieces of the things the Savior was teaching his apostles. While they were eating, Jesus said quietly but loud enough for all to hear, "Verily I say unto you that one of you shall betray me." The silence in the room was deafening. My own thoughts raced as I began to wonder which of the apostles would be so cold as to betray Jesus. Surely, it must be Judas, I thought to myself. I was wondering if the other apostles were thinking the same thing when to my surprise, each of the apostles humbly asked the Savior, "Lord, is it I?"[79]

Their humility and sorrow was tangible. I felt ashamed that my thoughts had immediately been to question and judge others, while their first thoughts had been to look inward. Jesus did not immediately respond to each of their heavyhearted questions, but he allowed them to ponder and reflect on their own commitment to him.

I could not help but think of the times when I had doubted the Savior and had not been valiant in my testimony of him. I could see that all men had or would in some way betray the Savior by not remaining faithful to the things we knew were true. From the example of these humble apostles, I realized that each of us must take inventory of our own lives if we are to remain true to the Savior and his teachings.

As I gathered up some of the plates from the dinner, I saw Judas question the Savior, but I did not hear what was said. I only heard Jesus respond, "What thou doest, do quickly."[80] Shortly after their exchange, Judas left the feast. I was not sure about the reason, but I assumed that he left in order to tend to some business. Judas held the bag and was the one responsible for the financial concerns of the group, so I assumed it had something to do with money.

Shortly after Judas departed, Jesus beckoned me to him. He quietly asked that I bring him a large towel, a basin, and a pitcher of water. I quickly retrieved the items he requested. As dinner concluded, he laid aside his clothing and girded himself with the towel. He then poured some of the water into the basin and began to wash the feet of each of the apostles.

For a small moment, I felt uncomfortable watching the Savior perform a task usually relegated to the lowest of servants. Why would he, the greatest among all men, stoop to perform such a menial task, especially on a night celebrating the deliverance of Israel? He was the great deliverer! At one point I thought about forbidding him and assuming the task myself, but I knew that this was something he desired to do in order to instruct his apostles.

As he came to wash Peter's feet, Peter forbade him, saying, "Lord, dost thou wash my feet?"

Jesus answered and said unto him, "What I do thou knowest not now; but thou shalt know hereafter."

Peter said unto him, "Thou shalt never wash my feet."

Jesus answered him, "If I wash thee not, thou hast no part with me."

Then Peter replied, "Lord, not my feet only, but also my hands and my head."[81]

At this, the Savior smiled and assured Peter that washing his feet was sufficient. Jesus then handed me the towel and basin and clothed himself again in his garments. He sat again with his apostles and inquired, "Know ye what I have done to you? Ye call me Master and Lord: and ye say well; for so I am. If I then, your Lord and Master, have washed your feet; ye also ought to wash one another's feet. For I have given you an example, that ye should do as I have done to you."

"Verily, verily, I say unto you, The servant is not greater than his lord; neither he that is sent greater than he that sent him. If ye know these things, happy are ye if ye do them."[82]

The Savior's words penetrated deep into my heart. He had asked me to serve rather than to sit at the table, and I had felt demeaned and lowered in station. Yet he had willingly and lovingly served his brethren to teach all men that service is not something that we simply endure as a part of our life on earth so we can earn the right to live in the mansions God has prepared for us. Service is the very thing of which an exalted life is made. When one serves with a willing heart, service is not demeaning but exalting.

The Savior had served his apostles as a show of his divine love for them. I realized that a desire to serve and bless others is an attribute of divinity. I also came to understand that when compelled and done without love, service is slavery. When we love others and serve willingly, we are truly free.

Chapter 19

Peace and the New Covenant

The Savior continued to teach his apostles while I helped my wife and in-laws clear the dishes and the remains of the feast. I was only able to hear bits and pieces of his instructions to them, but what I was able to hear filled my soul with joy and gladness. He spoke of the mansions of his Father, which he was going to prepare for all who followed him and stated, "I am the way, the truth, and the life."[83]

As I descended the stairs with a load of dishes, I reflected on his words. In following the Savior's way these last three years, I had come to know him. Not only were his teachings true, but he was also truth. Truth radiated from every fiber of his being. His way of living truly brought joy and happiness to my life. Though I had struggled at times to live the things that he taught, I had found that all that he said was true. My life had been more abundant and fulfilled when I lived as he taught.

I quickly returned to the upper room to gather more dishes and to catch more of what the Savior was teaching. As I entered the room, I heard him say, "But the Comforter, which is the Holy Ghost, whom the Father will send in my name, he shall teach you all things, and bring all things to your remembrance, whatsoever I have said unto you. Peace I leave with you, my peace I give unto you: not as the world giveth, give I unto you. Let not your heart be troubled, neither let it be afraid."[84]

At the time, I did not understand what he spoke regarding the Holy Ghost, but I did understand his teaching of peace. That is what I felt whenever I was near the Savior or followed his teachings—an inner peace that left me without doubt, worry, or concern about myself but rather filled me with love for others and a desire to be united with them through the love we all felt coming from the Savior. This peace I can only describe as a knowing, a certainty that the path that I have been following is indeed the right path, the one that will lead me to become all that God wants me to be and all that I desire in my heart to become.

As we were clearing the meal and bringing the last cup of wine that follows the Passover meal, Jesus asked me to bring him a small loaf of bread. I quickly retrieved a loaf from downstairs and brought it to him. He thanked me, but as he did so, I noticed something in his eye that I had not seen before. The only way to describe it was a sad kindness. I know that sounds ridiculous, but I felt as if he was about to do something that he wanted to do but was also saddened in doing.

Reverently and deliberately, Jesus took of the loaf of bread, broke it into small pieces, and placed them on a small plate. He then meekly bowed his head and blessed the bread with words that touched my soul. He took the plate and offered a piece to each of the apostles, telling them, "Take, eat; this is my body which is given for you: this do in remembrance of me." He then took the cup after supper and said, "This cup is the new testament in my blood, which is shed for many for the remission of sins."[85]

The spirit of what Jesus said and the solemnity of his offering to the apostles seemed to transcend any words I might use to describe it. The bread and wine seemed holy and sanctified by his offering. I stood pondering on the singularity of what I had witnessed. I could tell that each of the apostles were in deep reflection, thinking about what he had said and done. Jesus sat silent for several moments, allowing them to ponder this in their hearts.

My thoughts raced quickly to the experience that my wife and I shared as Jesus had taught his sermon about the Bread of Life. The thought came with great force that the bread and the wine were being given by the Savor to fulfill and replace the symbols of the Passover. The bread was the symbol to replace the lamb, making Jesus both the Bread of Life and the Lamb to be slain. My heart ached. I felt as I did when I first realized that Jesus was going to be sacrificed, though he was as innocent as a lamb. I fought against the idea. I didn't want to believe that such a powerful and good man could ever be taken and put to death.

I had watched him perform many miracles to bless so many lives. Surely, God would provide another way as he had done in order to save Isaac in former days, sparing Abraham the grief of having to sacrifice his son. Surely, I thought God will provide an escape and spare him until he had accomplished a full and joyful life, a life such as the one that he had made possible for me.

As I pondered these things, the Savior spoke once again. Quietly, reverently, but with great intensity, he addressed his apostles. "I am the vine, ye are the branches; without me ye can do nothing. He that abideth in me, and I in him, the same bringeth forth much fruit: for without me ye can do nothing. If ye abide in me, and my words abide in you, ye shall ask what ye will, and it shall be done unto you. Herein is my Father glorified, that ye bear much fruit; so shall ye be my disciples."[86]

Jesus went on to speak of his Father's love for him because he had kept his commandments. He admonished his apostles to keep his commandments so that they might abide in his love just as he had kept the commandments of his Father and abided in his love. He reminded them that the great commandment was to love one another. Then Jesus spoke words that left me with a foreboding feeling of impending sorrow. "Greater love hath no man than this, that a man lay down his life for his friends. Ye are my friends, if ye do whatsoever I command you."[87]

I descended the stairs to find my wife busily tending to the duties of the kitchen. I tenderly approached her and put my hands about her shoulders, gently pressing my cheek to her soft brown hair and whispering in her ear how much I loved her. She turned to see tears in my eyes as the realization of what was ahead overwhelmed me. She embraced me and inquired about my tears. I gently walked with her to another part of the house and told her of the things Jesus had shared with his apostles. I told her that I now knew beyond question that Jesus had come to Jerusalem to give himself to those who desired to kill him. He was going to lay down his life for all of us.

Tears began to well up in her eyes as she whispered, "Are you sure? Are you certain that you have not misunderstood? Perhaps he was speaking these things as a parable as he has done so many times before?" I assured her that I was certain, recounting as near as I could the Savior's exact words about his great love for us and his willingness to lay down his life for his friends. Her questioning gaze turned to complete sadness, and we embraced each other.

I suggested that we go back to the upper room to listen to the Savior's words before he departed, but my wife felt like she should return to help in the kitchen. I assured her that the dishes could wait but that this may be the last time that we would be able to listen to Jesus before he would allow himself to be taken by the Sanhedrin. She agreed, and we quickly but quietly made our way up the stairs to the upper room.

As we were about to enter, we could hear Jesus praying. We stopped outside the door and listened. Jesus's words pierced the heavens, and I felt certain that he communed directly with God, whom he addressed only as his Father.

I could not make out all that he said, but I could tell that he was praying very intimately for the apostles. Then as if he knew that we were listening at the door, he expanded his pleadings to include all who would believe in him through the teachings of the apostles.

"Neither pray I for these alone, but for them also which shall believe on me through their word; that they all may be one; as thou, Father, art in me, and I in thee, that they also may be one in us: that the world may believe that thou hast sent me. And the glory which thou gavest me I have given them; that they may be one, even as we are one: I in them, and thou in me, that they may be made perfect in one; and that the world may know that thou hast sent me, and hast loved them, as thou hast loved me. Father, I will that they also, whom thou hast given me, be with me where I am; that they may behold my glory, which thou hast given me: for thou lovedst me before the foundation of the world."[88]

The power of his words swept through me as the morning light sweeps away the darkness of the night. It seemed to energize and give life to every fiber of my being. Though I did not fully comprehend or understand what he meant when he prayed for us to be one, I knew that I felt empowered and able to do all that God asked of me. I longed to physically embrace him and be one with him.

Standing in the doorway, the Spirit bore witness to my soul again that he was indeed God's Son, who would save us. I did not understand, however, how we could be where he was and enjoy his glory if he was to be slain. I felt confused. I had been taught on more than one occasion that he was to be the Lamb who would be slain, but now I felt with even greater power that he was going to lift all of us to be one with him and with our Father in heaven. Did he expect all of us to give our lives with him in order to escape from the rule of the Romans? Surely, this could not be what he meant.

Following Jesus's prayer, I heard the apostles all join with Jesus to sing one of the beloved hymns from the psalmist. My wife and I watched as the apostles solemnly and reverently departed the upper room. Jesus paused, gently touched each of us on the arm, and looked lovingly into our eyes before following his disciples from the room. There was a look of gratitude yet also sadness as he departed. As my wife and I moved in to finish cleaning the room and gather the few remaining dishes, I could not help but wonder what this night would bring and what lay ahead for Jesus and his apostles.

Chapter 20

Visions of the Night

Those wonderings continued to fill my head and my heart as I finally retired for the evening. Sleep came quickly, but rest escaped me. My thoughts of Jesus soon became visions of the night. In my dreams I found myself in the garden of Gethsemane, a place where Jesus had often gone to contemplate and to pray. The garden was filled with olive trees and a large press resting in the center. Gethsemane, meaning "the oil press," had at one time been a place where olives were collected and crushed in the large stone press.

As I stood in the garden, I could see Jesus kneeling and praying. He seemed to be in terrible agony. I heard him plead as a child would cry unto his father, "Abba, Father, all things are possible unto thee; take away this cup from me: nevertheless not what I will, but what thou wilt."[89]

The intensity of his pleading pierced my soul. I ached at his pain. I witnessed as he struggled with an unseen force upon him. His agony was more than I could bear to watch. Suddenly yet reassuringly, there was an angel at his side, embracing and comforting him. He spoke to Jesus in warm and tender tones, assuring him that he had been sent by the Father so that he would know his love and receive the strength and vision to endure. I could not hear all that was said, but I felt a love and presence that overwhelmed me. The countenance of the angel shone upon Jesus.

He gazed upon the angel for some time, and then he began to look about as if he were searching for someone.

As I followed Jesus's gaze about the garden, I could see an endless multitude of people. I was awestruck by the myriad of spirits who had come to be with the Savior. The words of the prophet Isaiah came flooding into my mind. "And when thou shalt make his soul an offering for sin, he shall see his seed."[90] These were his seed—all those who believed in him as their Redeemer and Savior. I could feel the combined faith of the mass of people surrounding me. Though the host of people seemed innumerable, it appeared as if Jesus was looking into the face and heart of each and every person.

As I looked about at the throng of people, I could not help but ask myself, "Am I his seed? Am I one of his faithful?" Then as if to respond to my ponderings, Jesus's gaze turned to me. In an instant my question was answered, and it was as if we were completely alone together in the garden. As he looked upon me, time seemed to stand still. I saw and felt every ache, every sorrow, and every sin that I had already and would yet experience during my life. I began to hurt in a way that I had never before experienced. Then tenderly, I felt the Savior's arms about me. He gazed into my eyes. His love seemed to envelop every part of my being, overcoming and enveloping every hurt, every heartache, and every pain of my life—not just those caused by sin but every pain or injustice brought upon me through my mortal journey.

As he embraced me, I felt all my pain leave. It was replaced by a joy and love that left me unable to speak. I wept for joy as he smiled upon me. In that moment, I understood what my Aramaic friends had told me about the "kafat" or embrace. They said that it was actually a sign of being at one with someone. It was this unity or "at-one-ment" that I felt in that moment with Jesus.

With a gentle touch on my arm and one last knowing look in my eyes, Jesus moved on to visit with others who had come to the garden. As Jesus took time with each one, I felt their joy as if it had been my own. Time vanished, and all that mattered was Jesus's love and concern for every person who had come to the garden. It was as if he was becoming one with each person, lifting the burdens of every one of us as his brothers and sisters, taking our burdens upon himself.

After an eternity that felt as but a few moments, he walked to where Peter, James, and John lay fast asleep. Without the least feeling of scorn or rebuke, he gently roused them and asked them if they could not watch with him for an hour. I half-smiled to myself, thinking how exhausted they must be after a full meal and a long night of waiting. Even the most devout disciple would find it hard to fight the overwhelming desire for sleep.

The Savior returned to pray again to his father. As he prayed this second time, I noticed that while close to the words he had first spoken to his Father, this time he seemed to pray with greater earnestness, determined now to drink of the bitter cup that was before him, knowing that in so doing, he would bring hope to all those who had come to express their faith and love for him. For the joy of the redemption that he would provide for his brothers and sisters, he endured suffering to satisfy the demands of justice. His will was now in line with that of his Father as he prayed, "O my Father, if this cup may not pass away from me, except I drink it, thy will be done."[91]

The spirit in the garden intensified. The sorrow of every soul and all the agonies of eternity seemed to be pressing upon Jesus. I sensed his pain, his all-consuming agony. He seemed to be struggling to resist the crushing weight he had taken from each one, not allowing the bitterness that he had born to enter his heart, not allowing it to overcome his divine nature and change his character or the nature of his being. He groaned in his striving against sin.

Then I saw it. In the dimness of the moonlight, I could see that the tunic next to his body began to darken. Then his robe took on the appearance of a deep crimson. I was horrified as I realized that his pleadings to resist sin had left him bleeding from the very pores of his body![92]

Suddenly, I shot upright in my bed. My heart raced within me. A dream? Or had this been real? The sorrow in my heart left me heaving with a sadness that would not leave. I began to weep from the very core of my being. I tried to tell myself that it was just a dream, but my heart would not believe what my head was trying to persuade me to accept.

"This could not be real," I almost shouted in my mind. Even if Christ had gone to Gethsemane, surely not all of humanity had assembled to witness the suffering I saw in my mind's eye. The logic of my mind began to calm the dread that was in my heart.

A dream. Just a dream.

As I gathered in my surroundings, I realized that my pillow was wet with the tears that I had shed during my dreams of the night. Gradually, I began to think back upon the joy of the evening spent in the upper chamber of my father-in-law's home when Jesus had prayed with such tenderness that we would all be one with him and with the Father. The thought of this joyful union calmed my heart. Had he not promised his disciples peace as he had spoken with them in the upper room? I thought on his words, "Peace I leave with you, my peace I give unto you: not as the world give I unto you. Let not your heart be troubled, neither let it be afraid."[93] The thoughts of his peace calmed my heart and allowed me to put the dream from my mind long enough to fall into a restful sleep.

Chapter 21

Denials and Trials

My wife awakened me well before dawn. There was an urgency in her voice as she whispered, "Come! Something is happening with Jesus." I hurriedly dressed and went with her to the front salon of her parents' home, where one of their friends from the Sanhedrin named Nicodemus was speaking with them in very somber tones. We slowly entered the room. The grave look on my father-in-law's face spoke volumes.

"They have taken him, Son," he said. "Judas betrayed Jesus to the council, and they have taken him to the hall of Caiaphas. They are putting him on trial for blasphemy. They intend to have him killed."

Though Jesus had prophesied to us that his life would be taken, this news brought a chill of horror and sadness that left me without breath. I embraced my wife, who then began to cry. Her mother gently put her arm around her, and we all wept. I looked into the eyes of Nicodemus.

"Is there nothing that can be done?" I inquired.

His gaze dropped to the floor, and he slowly shook his head. "I am afraid that they are determined to have him killed. I have heard them say that they will accuse him of sedition and take him before Pilate to be crucified."

Again, horror shot through me. Crucified! Of all the deaths to suffer, this was the most cruel and painful. Surely, God would intervene. Jesus was his Son. I knew this with every fiber of my being. Surely, God would not allow these wicked men to crucify his Son. Though I had finally allowed myself to believe and acknowledge Jesus's words that he would sacrifice his life to save us, I could not bring myself to believe that God would allow his Son to face death in such an agonizing way. My mind raced.

"I must go to the hall," I said resolutely.

"There is nothing that can be done," Nicodemus insisted.

"Perhaps not," I replied, "but I want to be there with him regardless of what they do." My wife agreed that we should go, so we quickly made our way to the great hall of the high priest.

I heard the cock crowing in the distance as we approached the courtyard outside of the great hall. The sun was just beginning to break over the horizon. As we approached, I saw a man standing a short distance outside the gate. As we neared him, I recognized that it was Peter. He was weeping uncontrollably. There was a bitterness to his sobs that seemed to overshadow the sadness of his lament. My voice trembled as I took him by the shoulders. "Is it done?" I blurted. "Have they killed the Lord?"

Peter slowly shook his head. "Not yet, but they have put him on trial for blasphemy." Then he stuttered through gasping sobs, "He said that I would deny him, but I was certain that I would stand at his side no matter what they did to me. And now I have lost my soul. I have denied knowing him not once but three times. Oh, how can I ever stand before God?" He grasped me about my shoulders and looked pleadingly into my eyes. "I once stood and witnessed to all that he is indeed the Christ and God's own Son. Now I have denied even knowing him! What have I done!"

Before I could offer any type of consolation, he continued his lamentation, "After the last time that I denied him, Jesus looked upon me, and I thought that my very heart would break for the sadness that I saw in his eyes. It was as if he was hurting for me, not for himself. How could I have denied such love?"

He looked about as if searching for some answer, some reason for his weakness in this time of trial. I could feel his anguish, doubt, and despair.

"Why would he tell me with such force that I would deny him?" he muttered, almost to himself. "It was as if it was what he wanted me to do." Then as if trying to explain himself, he turned to us and said, "When they inquired of me about knowing him, the word no flew out of my lips before I could stop from denying what I knew to be true. I felt like I could not help myself. But now … now what am I to do? Surely, there is no way for me to undo that which I have done!"

At this he looked into my eyes as if to beg me for reassurance that he had not done that which Christ had said was unpardonable. My wife reached out and gently stroked his arm. I took Peter to my bosom and embraced him, assuring him that Christ knows all things and that somehow even this denial was a part of what had to happen to bring about God's purposes. "So many times we see dimly what Jesus knows with great light and vision," I said. "Perhaps this experience will serve its purpose in some future day. We must have faith and trust that Jesus would not declare your denial if he did not know of its importance in the events that must transpire for him to fulfill the Father's plan for all of us."

These words seemed to give Peter a feeling of hope. He put his arm upon my shoulder and looked at me, tears still glistening in his eyes. Yet now I saw in those eyes what seemed to be a flicker of hope. He patted me gently on the back of my head and pulled me to him. We again embraced before parting ways. He moved slowly back toward Gethsemane as my wife and I made our way to the great hall. I was certain that Peter still had his own garden of growth and understanding to face and weeds yet to be overcome to gain his own fruit of forgiveness and reconciliation.

As my wife and I entered the great hall, we slipped silently among the gathering crowd to observe the proceedings. We saw Jesus standing in the middle of the room, blindfolded and bound. The Sanhedrin guards were slapping him in the face and mocking him. "Prophesy, who is it that smote thee?"[94] They spit in his face and spoke all manner of filthiness against him. The crowd joined in the derision of Jesus, yet he stood calm and resolute, a majestic figure of dignity and peace in the face of a raging storm of hatred and bitterness. I marveled at the peace that filled Jesus despite the conflict and turmoil about him. It reminded me of the time when he stood serenely on the boat, commanding, "Peace, be still!" This time he seemed to be speaking the words to his own soul rather than to the tumultuous Sea of Galilee. He appeared unaffected by the behavior of those around him, determined not to let their anger and bitterness inside of his own soul. It was just as I had witnessed him endure in my dreams.

From the doorway above the court, the Sanhedrin entered the room. The crowd began to quiet themselves as the chief priests questioned Jesus. "Art thou the Christ? Tell us."

He said unto them, "If I tell you, ye will not believe. And if I also ask you, ye will not answer me, nor let me go. Hereafter shall the Son of Man sit on the right hand of the power of God."

Then said they all, "Art thou then the Son of God?"

And he said unto them, "Ye say that I am."[95]

Then the high priest rent his clothes, saying, "He hath spoken blasphemy; what further need have we of witnesses? behold, now ye have heard his blasphemy. What think ye?"

The members of the Sanhedrin court answered almost in unison, "He is guilty of death."[96]

I stood filled with mixed and confused emotions. Anger swelled up in me toward these men who pretended to be so religious. Were they so cold and hard-hearted that they could not see the goodness in Jesus? Yet I also found myself troubled that Jesus had not stood up to them and rebuked them as he had rebuked the stormy seas of Galilee. I had witnessed his power over demons and storms of every kind. Surely, he had the power to free himself and to stand strong against their vanity and villainy. But he just stood there—erect, calm, and peaceful as a morning following a stormy night. It was as if he had already fought and won this battle privately before ever facing the conflict publicly. I saw in him the peace of which he had spoken to his disciples in the upper room. He held his peace.

I suddenly realized that the peace that the Savior promised those who followed him was not the absence of conflict in their lives but the ability to stand before such conflict with peace in their souls that they were doing the will of God. With this peace firmly rooted in their hearts, nothing could dissuade them from behaving in a manner consistent with what God would have them do. Yes, there would be times when God would have them use the sword to overcome, but many times the battle would be fought in keeping the evil out of their hearts rather than removing the evil from their world.

Chapter 22

No King but Caesar

As I pondered these ideas inspired by the Savior's unconquerable calm, my wife nudged my arm and whispered, "They are taking them to Pilate. Should we follow?"

I was quickly brought back to the matters of the moment. The whole multitude was pushing and thronging their way to take Jesus before Pilate, the Roman governor over Jerusalem and the surrounding area. My wife and I quickly joined in the short journey to the court of the Roman leadership. At first, Pilate seemed uninterested in the dealings of the Jews with one who had violated their religious beliefs, but the Sanhedrin assured Pilate, ""We found this fellow perverting the nation, and forbidding to give tribute to Caesar, saying that he himself is Christ a King."[97]

This seemed to draw Pilate's interest. He began to question Jesus, who again stood calm and unruffled in the face of this Roman ruler. "Art thou the King of the Jews?" he inquired.

"Thou sayest it,"[98] Jesus replied. Pilate seemed genuinely impressed at the manner of Jesus's demeanor and candid answers to his queries.

After several moments and a myriad of questions, Pilate stated, "I find no fault in this man."[99] I felt a sigh of relief pass through me as I heard his words. My wife, feeling the same relief, grasped my arm and hugged herself into me. I returned her embrace. Without

Roman sanction, the Sanhedrin may be able to denounce Jesus, but they could not put him to death.

This infuriated the Jewish leaders. They became even fiercer, claiming that Jesus was stirring up the people in the Jewish nation, beginning with the area of Galilee. Hearing that Jesus had preached in Galilee, Pilate inquired, "Is he a Galilean?" When they answered in the affirmative, Pilate immediately ordered that Jesus be taken to Herod, the governor of Galilee, who was in Jerusalem for the Passover.[100] I felt certain that Pilate wanted nothing to do with the judging of Jesus.

The Sanhedrin followed the Roman soldiers who had been assigned to take Jesus before Herod, ensuring that Jesus was condemned for his heresy against the Jewish nation. My wife and I followed at a distance. Herod was a churlish and vile man who pretended his allegiance to both Rome and the Jewish people. He had ordered John the Baptist beheaded at the request of his wife's daughter, and he was known for his cruelty. I feared what he might do to Jesus.

Herod questioned Jesus and demanded that he perform some type of miracle, but Jesus kept silent, neither speaking nor even acknowledging Herod. The Sanhedrin continued to deride and accuse Jesus, but he remained calm and unaffected by their rants and tirades. Herod attempted several times to get Jesus to say or do anything, but he only became more exasperated that he was being ignored by a common carpenter from Galilee. He smugly turned Jesus over to his guards, who abused Jesus and mocked him as a false and pretend king. Finally, Herod had had enough of their sport and sent Jesus back to Pilate.

Determined to see Jesus killed, the Sanhedrin again followed the soldiers back to Pilate, who seemed irritated and upset that Jesus had again been brought before him. He stated numerous times that he found no fault in Jesus or anything worthy of death in him. Pilate tried several times to appease the leaders and yet release this man whom he knew to be innocent. He offered to release a prisoner to the people in honor of their Passover, giving the people the option of releasing Jesus or Barabbas, a known murderer and thief. The crowd maliciously refused Jesus and called for Barabbas to be released.[101]

Reluctantly, Pilate commanded his men to scourge Jesus. They stripped him, beat him, plaited a crown of thorns that they pressed upon his head, clothed him in a purple robe, and then mocked him as a king. Hoping this would placate the people, Pilate brought him forth and proclaimed, "Behold the man!"[102]

I could not bear the scene before me. I turned my face away and pulled my wife to me, who was weeping openly. Jesus looked absolutely weakened and submissive. The words of the prophet Isaiah came vividly to my mind. "When we shall see him, there is no beauty that we should desire him. He is despised and rejected of men; a man of sorrows, and acquainted with grief: and we hid as it were our faces from him; he was despised, and we esteemed him not. Surely he hath borne our griefs, and carried our sorrows: yet we did esteem him stricken, smitten of God, and afflicted."[103] I thought that seeing Jesus in such a wretched and disgraced condition would be enough to appease the people who had come to behold the spectacle of Jesus's demise.

But I was mistaken. Suddenly, we heard someone cry out for him to be crucified. It was as Nicodemus had said. Nothing but Christ's crucifixion would satisfy their thirst for his blood. Pilate again tried to convince the leaders that Jesus had done nothing worthy of death. His pleas fell on deaf ears and hardened hearts.

A man whom I recognized from the day when Jesus had come triumphant into Jerusalem approached me. "You were there when we hailed Jesus as our Savior," he half-stated and half-inquired. "Why does he not defend himself? If he is our Messiah, why does he not stand up against Pilate? I do not understand." Several people around him began to ask similar questions. "I have followed him from the beginning," said one woman. "I trusted him and believed him to be the Messiah. I followed him here to Pilate to see him rise up and break the Roman bands, not only for himself but for all of us. We have seen his power. Surely, he is the one sent to set us free."

Before I could reply, a member of the Sanhedrin stepped in among our group and said, "Don't you see? He has lied to you! He has deceived you into following him that he might be lifted above you and bring you into his own yoke of bondage. He is not Messiah! He has led you to a false hope. Surely, Rome will respond to his sedition and make our burdens worse. He must die. He must be crucified! Crucify him! Crucify him!" he began to shout aloud.

The feeling of betrayal ran through the crowd like a wave of the sea rushing to the shore. I could feel the hate growing among the throng, which quickly became a mob of disgruntled, angry citizens. Suddenly, all the people around us joined in the cry of the Sanhedrin. "Crucify him!" they echoed. The chants became louder and louder as more people joined in the demand to have Jesus crucified. The pleas of my wife and me to stop this madness became drowned out in the sea of anger and bitterness leveled toward Jesus. They felt that he had deceived them and given them false hope—a hope that they now saw being dashed before the power of Rome. The crowd jeered at the sorrowful submissiveness of the man they had once believed would set them free.

Pilate tried again to obtain release for Jesus, answering the crowds cry for crucifixion with the simple question, "Why, what evil hath he done? I have found no cause of death in him: I will therefore chastise him, and let him go."[104]

This brought the crowd to a fever pitch, and they responded, "If thou let this man go, thou art not Cæsar's friend: whosoever maketh himself a king speaketh against Cæsar."[105]

Pilate stood troubled and perplexed. He had Jesus brought forth, beaten, bloodied, and adorned with the cruel crown of thorns and the false robe of a king. "Behold, your king! Shall I crucify your king?" he asked.

Pilate's question was answered by a cry from the crowd that shook my heart and left me in disbelief. "We have no King but Caesar!"[106] I could not believe my ears. This people who had fought against the harsh bondage of Rome for years was now confessing Caesar himself to be their ruler while rejecting God and his Son as their rightful King. Surely, they did not understand what they were saying, but they were caught up in the malignant madness stirred up by the Sanhedrin. The cry for crucifixion grew louder.

Pilate motioned to one of his servants. For a brief instant, I hoped that he might go against the crowd and follow what he knew in his heart to be the right thing to do. He alone had power to stand up against the mob of injustice and hatred. To my disappointment, his servant brought a pitcher of water and a small basin. Nodding to his servant, Pilate then began to wash his hands as the servant poured water from the pitcher into the basin. Pilate then wiped his hands and said, "I am innocent of the blood of this just person: see ye to it."[107] I could not help but think that a man's hands were never dirtier than at this moment of acquiescence.

To my astonishment, the people responded to Pilate's gesture with one accord, "His blood be on us, and on our children."[108] My heart seemed to crush under the defiant and willing acceptance of their own cruelty and condemnation. I could not believe that they would encourage such anger and bitterness upon the heads of their future posterity. I turned to my wife, whose face reflected the horror that I felt, standing among a people who so openly rejected the Son of God. Surely, the heavens wept as we did at such utter hatred and lack of remorse.

Chapter 23

Lessons from the Cross

Delivering Jesus to the desires of the ruthless crowd, Pilate commanded that he be led away to be crucified. The Roman soldiers took a large cross and laid it upon his back, compelling him to carry it toward Golgotha, known as the place of the skull.

My wife and I watched helplessly as he struggled under the heavy burden he had to bear. Weakened by all that he had been required to endure, he fought to move forward. The soldiers mocked and beat him as he walked until he finally collapsed under the tremendous load of all that had been placed upon him. As I moved forward to lift the cross from the Savior, the soldiers grabbed another man from among the crowd and compelled him to carry the cross. They then lifted Jesus to his feet and forced him to follow as they pushed forward to Calvary.

We joined several other disciples of Jesus as we followed him along this way of pain to his destined demise. I recognized John standing among several of the women whom I had seen with the Savior on various occasions. Some of the women began to weep and lament as they called out to Jesus. He turned to them, and with a voice filled with compassion, he said, "Daughters of Jerusalem, weep not for me, but weep for yourselves, and for your children. For, behold, the days are coming, in the which they shall say, Blessed are the barren, and the wombs that never bare, and the paps which never gave suck. Then shall they begin to say to the mountains, Fall on us; and to the hills, Cover us."[109]

I marveled that even in this time of his great pain and suffering, Jesus's thoughts were for others—not just those who stood as witnesses to his sufferings but also those who would remain behind to see the great calamities that were yet to come upon the people and their posterity. In every way and at all times, he continued to live what he taught—to think first of others and forget oneself. How could he keep such perspective of life when all around him seemed to have forgotten or outright denied who he was?

The next several moments seemed surreal. It was as if my mind would not allow me to fully comprehend the agony of what was happening. I could not bear to watch as the soldiers nailed him to the cross. First his hands and then his wrists and finally his feet were nailed into place with the long spikes used by the soldiers. Each driving blow of their mallet seemed to pierce my heart with unspeakable sorrow. When Jesus was finally lifted up between two others who had been sentenced to crucifixion atop Calvary's hill, my wife and I stood among the other disciples, weeping hopelessly for our friend and brother. No words can describe the emptiness and agony of what we witnessed.

I stood helplessly by as the Roman soldiers parted his raiment and cast lots for his cloak. I felt anger and hatred begin to swell up in me toward these men as they mocked the man I had grown to love. Then looking to heaven, Jesus said in a loving tone that overwhelmed my anger, "Father, forgive them; for they know not what they do."[110] I could not believe my ears. How could he forgive them for such coldhearted cruelty?

As I gazed upon him, thoughts of his teachings on the mount came echoing into my mind. "Love your enemies, bless them that curse you, do good to them that hate you, and pray for them which despitefully use you, and persecute you."[111]

When I had heard Jesus speak these words in the calm of that peaceful afternoon almost three years earlier, I thought how divine and soothing they had sounded in my ear. It was easy to agree with Jesus in that magnificent moment of love and communion from atop the mountainside. Yet hearing his words of love and forgiveness from the cross toward those who had placed him there came as a hammer to an anvil. His words caused me to contemplate whether I could truly love my enemies and bless those who cursed me. It seemed an impossible task, and yet here was Jesus, teaching me to forgive—not through just words—but through his deeds.

Witnessing this incredible scene, a stroke of revealing light flashed upon my mind. Forgiveness is actually made possible because of what Jesus suffered! Even in his hour of agony, he found the strength to live the law of love and forgiveness, giving to each of us the chance to be forgiven. If we would turn our hearts to him and accept his atoning sacrifice, we would see his love and mercy were sufficient to save all who would repent. His plea of forgiveness reminded me that while these soldiers were in every way heartless and cruel, they were unaware of the higher law of love that Jesus lived and taught. By allowing himself to be taken and crucified, he was providing the very way for their forgiveness!

As I looked up into the face of Jesus, I could see a peace and calm in him despite his incredible pain. Truly, he was more than a man of wisdom, compassion, and love. His actions witnessed to me again that he was indeed the very Son of God. Yet as those thoughts of testimony came to my mind, I could not help but wonder why he, the very Son of God, would allow himself to be taken and treated with such contempt.

Then it hit me. Allowed! He allowed this to happen. All of this was not beyond his ability to control, but it was something that he had allowed to occur to teach us and show us how to endure the crosses that we, too, would have to bear, often at the hands of those who are filled with hatred and unrighteousness. To forgive and be forgiven requires faith in Jesus, not just in what he taught but in the fact that he truly is the Son of God.

Again, I was abruptly brought back from my place of pondering as one of the men hanging on a cross next to Jesus began to deride him and rail on him. As if throwing Jesus's divine calling in his face, the man chided, "If thou be Christ, save thyself and us."[112]

Then the man hanging on the other side of Jesus spoke, "Dost not thou fear God, seeing thou art in the same condemnation? And we indeed justly; for we receive the due reward of our deeds: but this man hath done nothing amiss." Then the man turned to Jesus and pleaded, "Lord, remember me when thou comest into thy kingdom."

Jesus responded, "Verily I say unto thee, To day shalt thou be with me in paradise."[113]

As so many previous times throughout my journeys with Jesus, his words left me uncertain as to their meaning. As I contemplated his statement, his words in the upper room returned and brought light and understanding. "Father, I will that they also, whom thou hast given me, be with me where I am; that they may behold my glory, which thou hast given me: for thou lovedst me before the foundation of the world."[114]

This is what the Savior meant that we would be where he is to behold his glory. Death is not the end! Somehow, death would serve as a means for him to return to be with his Father and to enjoy the glory of paradise. Exactly how this was to happen, I was unsure, but Jesus's words to the man on the cross witnessed to my soul that his death would somehow open a doorway for all of us to return to God and be with him again. It allowed me to see the cross in a whole new light. Rather than being an instrument of Christ's death, it became in my mind a symbol that death was not the end but the beginning of a paradisiacal life in which we would behold the glory of Jesus as the Son of God.

I turned to share my newfound understanding with my wife, who was standing close to the other disciples who had come to the cross. I moved near to them and saw John standing close by one of the more elderly women in the group. I thought that I had recognized her. I embraced John, who then introduced me to Mary, the mother of Jesus. As I looked into her eyes, the years seemed to melt away, and I reflected on that night in Bethlehem when she had introduced me to her newborn son. So much had transpired in the intervening years, yet when she looked into my eyes, she said, "I am sorry, but you look vaguely familiar. Have we met before?"

"Many years ago," I replied. "Under much different circumstances. You introduced me to your newborn son as you raised him from his bed of straw in a lowly manger."

Suddenly, her eyes lit up with a knowing and recognition that touched my heart. "The shepherd boy!" she cried. She placed her hands about my face and smiled. Her hands were so gentle and tender and her love was so real that it warmed my heart. I knew that her heart must be breaking at the sight of her dear son dying upon the cross. I longed to share what I had just learned about his death, but I could not find the words. I simply embraced her and expressed my sorrow at her pain.

As we all looked up to Jesus upon the cross, he gazed first at his mother and then to John, his beloved disciple to whom he had been so close. He then looked back to his mother and said tenderly, "Woman, behold thy son." Then he said to John, "Behold thy mother."[115] Nodding his awareness as to Jesus's wishes, John put his arm around Mary and held her close.

Once again, I found myself marveling at the example of Jesus. Even in this time of his ultimate pain and sorrow, his thoughts were not for himself but for those he loved. I thought of the many times in my own life when I had become selfish and self-absorbed as I faced difficulty and distress. Now from the cross of his affliction, he was showing me how to forget myself and think of others. Jesus not only talked the talk of selfless concern but walked the walk, even when that walk led him down a difficult road, namely the painful path of perfection.

Chapter 24

Atonement and "Alone-ment"

The day passed as we huddled together for some type of consolation. Watching as Jesus suffered on the cross was almost unbearable, but it seemed to be all that we could do. In the middle of the day, a darkness spread over the land that completely blocked the sun. It was as if all creation was mourning the death of God's beloved Son, the very Creator himself. He had said at the feast that he was sent to be the light to the world, but now that light was being removed—overcome by the darkness of bitterness, anger, and hatred. I tried to recall the light that had come into my mind in hearing his statement about paradise, but it was as if the darkness was extinguishing any light or hope that I had felt. My head continued to tell me that this is what he prophesied and that it had to be, but that did not ease the ache and pain in my heart. I held my wife close as we both sobbed at the intense sorrow we felt. Storms began to rage as all creation joined in our sorrow and despair.

When all light seemed to have vanished and the darkness had become all-consuming, I heard the Savior cry with a loud voice, "My God, my God! Why hast thou forsaken me?"[116] The pain and loneliness in his voice were heart-wrenching. I felt as if I could not breath, as if all life had been swept from my soul. Surely, God, his Father, had not abandoned Jesus in his greatest moment of need! Why would he have left him alone to die? Could he not have sent his Spirit or angels to give him some comfort to endure the final agonies of death?

In all my contact with Jesus, I had never known him to be without the Spirit of his Father. I remembered his words to the disciples in the upper room that he was not alone because the Father was always with him.[117] Why had the Father left him alone in the greatest hour of his need? I thought back to the feeling of abandonment I felt when the sorrows of my first wife's death left me without hope and without light. The darkness and loneliness had been overwhelming

Then as if a ray of sunlight pierced through the darkness of the day, understanding came into my darkened mind. He had to know. Jesus had to know the utter aloneness that all of us would feel so that he could comprehend all things and be able to give us strength in the times when we would feel alone. Thus, through his atonement we would never experience an "alone-ment" as long as we remembered the cross and his suffering in order to know and experience all that we could experience in life. As he had ascended up on high, so he had to descend below all so that he might be in and through all things the light of truth. He alone could now shine a light into the darkest moments of our lives and help us see our way to be one with him and with the Father just as he had prayed with his apostles in the upper room of my father-in-law's home. He was not only at one with the Father, but he was now at one with us in every possible way.

I was overwhelmed at the light that came into my mind, and while I was filled with joy in knowing that we would never have to be alone again, I wept at the price Jesus had to pay to become one with us so that he could make us one with the Father. In that moment, the cross became a symbol of the price he paid to become one with us and the promise that we would never be alone unless we chose to ignore his sacrifice for us. Alone becomes at-one because of the cross which Christ endured.

Forgiveness, life, love, and loneliness—these were powerful lessons taught in a most unexpected way and in the most unlikely circumstance. Even in his final moments, Jesus was a teacher for all who would observe, ponder, and see by the Spirit of truth and light.

As these thoughts came peacefully into my mind, I saw a calmness and clarity come into the face of Jesus. He glanced upward and almost whispered, "Father, it is finished! Into thy hands I commend my spirit."[118] With that he bowed his head, heaved one last sigh, and released his spirit from the agony of his pain-filled body. All in our little group began to cry once again, knowing that it was indeed finished. I again embraced my wife as we both shuddered under the agony of the moment.

His final words echoed in my mind. "Into thy hands I commend my spirit." Again, amid the unconscionable, understanding came into my mind. Jesus was going home! His Father had not completely abandoned him. For those few brief moments, God had left Jesus alone to allow him to comprehend our feelings of loneliness, but now the Father stood ready to receive him into the mansions of which he had spoken while in the upper room. I could imagine in my mind the joy of that reunion as the Father of us all reached out to embrace his obedient Son.

While I pictured in my mind's eye that moment of joyful reunion, the reality of what had just happened and the sobbing of all around me pulled me back to the present. Jesus's body hung lifeless on the cross. He had gone to join his father, but what of us? His journey and mission seemed at an end, but what was ahead for those of us who had come to love and trust in him? Where were we to go? What were we to do?

"It is finished." The finality of those words seemed as a reverberating echo in my mind, closing any door of hope or light that I had in my heart. The lessons that I had just learned seemed to vanish from my mind and my heart. I tried desperately to hold on to what I had just felt and learned, but I seemed to be sinking helplessly into the hopelessness that surrounded me. His life was ended. His story was now complete. With all the imaginings of my mind, I could not bring him back to life. The pain, the suffering, the agony—it truly was now finished.

The darkness of the moment enveloped me and a sense of utter despair and emptiness seemed to seep into my heart. I tried desperately to hold on to some small measure of the hope and light that I had realized in the process of his sacrifice, but I was unable to see through the death of the man who had been my light for most of my life. All the memories of his miracles in my life slipped silently into the darkness of my despair. The lessons I had just learned seemed to be simple meanderings of my mind. Reality proved to be an overwhelming argument against the hope I had allowed into my heart and mind. All hope appeared to disappear as the distant mist of a morning meadow.

In my despair, my sorrow shifted. I no longer wept for Jesus, but I thought only of myself, my wife, and all those who had faithfully followed Jesus. I held my wife, grasping for any kind of hope or light to lift me from the depths of my sorrow, but all seemed hopeless. John held Mary. All around us seemed lost and alone. Faith seemed to fade into the reality that Jesus was no longer with us. There would be no miraculous hand to reach into our souls and heal our broken hearts. The healer was taken from us, and we could not be consoled. The finality of that Friday seemed as dreadful as the darkness that had consumed the light of day.

Chapter 25

Light amidst the Darkness

The next moments were a blur. I remember the soldiers coming to break Jesus's legs to hasten his death, but when they found him already dead, they instead pierced his side with a sword. Nicodemus came a few moments later with another man I did not know, and they took the body of Jesus to a tomb. My wife and I watched as they sealed the tomb with a large stone. As the stone was rolled into place, I felt as if a part of my heart became sealed off from the light and love that I had known.

We slowly and somberly made our way back to the home of her parents. The emotions of the day had taken their toll upon us. The Sabbath was beginning, but we felt no desire to partake of the evening meal. As we sat recounting the events of the day to my wife's parents, I tried desperately to remember all the insights and flashes of light that I had experienced, but they all seemed to be swallowed up in the despair that now enveloped my heart. There was no peace, no understanding breaking through to give me hope or to bring light to my now darkened mind.

I grasped for anything upon which to rekindle my faith. Had he not said that he would give himself for a sacrifice? I had believed his teachings. I had received witnesses of his divine Sonship. Now all my feelings of faith seemed swallowed up in a sea of doubt. I was sinking into the waters of my own fears. Why could I not accept and believe him? Had I really known the truth? Was he truly the Messiah? Was he truly the Son of God?

Perhaps I had just been drawn in by his personality, his charisma, and his love. Perhaps all that I had felt and all that I had experienced were simply the imaginations of my mind and the naïve wishes of a heart hoping to be part of something miraculous. The more I reached for faith, the more I felt empty. Fear began to join with my doubt, and I found myself trembling at all that I had lost.

My wife came and sat by me and touched my arm. I looked up to meet her gaze. She must have seen the sadness I was feeling, yet I did not see in her eyes the despair and doubt that had gripped my own heart.

"We must continue to believe," she whispered.

"In what?" I almost shouted. "He is dead. In what are we to believe? God has abandoned us and left us utterly alone. There is no hope in Israel or a mystical Messiah. We are destined to be in bondage forever."

My words seemed to cut into the hopeful heart of my dear wife. "I know that this is hard to understand," she replied, "but I also know the healing that I received in a simple touch of this man's robes. I cannot deny what I know to be true. I trust in the witnesses that have been born in my heart. Do you not remember all that we have seen and all that we have felt?"

She looked into my eyes as if hoping to see any sign of belief. I returned her gaze, hoping to remember, but I found myself too confused and exhausted to think clearly. She sensed my discouragement.

"Perhaps a night of rest and a peaceful Sabbath will help to restore some sense of hope to your heart," she offered. I agreed that we needed rest. We excused ourselves from her parents and retired for the evening. Thankfully, my exhaustion overwhelmed me, and sleep came quickly and completely.

It was the middle of the morning when my wife finally awakened me with a gentle nudge.

"We are going to the synagogue to celebrate Shabbat," she said. "I was hoping that you might come with us to worship."

"Worship what?" I replied. "There is nothing to celebrate. All that we have believed, all that we have practiced—it is all meaningless. I believed Jesus to be the Messiah. I was certain of it. But now he is as lifeless as my hopes and my faith. I had hoped that the morning would bring light again to my mind, but I realize now that without him, there is no light."

"But there is light," my wife insisted. "The light of his teachings, the light of his love. Those are real and can remain with us forever if we will just give place in our hearts to believe him. He may not be among us, but we can keep his memory alive in our hearts by loving as he loved and living as he lived. Faith is not to understand and know all things but to live with hope for the future based upon the evidence of what we have seen in the past. Do not forget all that you have witnessed in your life just because we are temporarily in the darkness. Just as the sun arises each day to chase the darkness of the night, I feel certain that by living his teachings, his light will spring up in us anew and bring us joy and peace. But you must choose to remember your experiences and move forward with faith. Focus on your faith, not your doubts. Doubt your doubts, not your faith-filled experiences."

Her words rang with an echo of the things Jesus had taught me months before when I had allowed doubt to come into my mind. They seemed to penetrate the darkness I had allowed into my heart. As I reflected on that experience, other memories of things I had learned and experiences with Jesus began to flood my mind with light. Suddenly, I could see again. It was as if the light of his countenance was radiating to me through the light of my wife's faith and hope. I could see that if I was to have faith to overcome my doubt, I had to put into action the things he had taught.

Living water began to pour into my soul. I felt renewed and restored. She was right! The only way to keep the Savior alive in my life was to live what he taught. I did not need to have him constantly by my side to know the joy of living his teachings. His words had taught me how to live and to love. They had brought me peace. The kind of life that I was going to live was now up to me. Every time I had chosen to live his words, I had found peace, joy, and light. Whenever I allowed my doubts to darken my faith and did not live his teachings, I fell into despair and destructive behavior. I now had to choose to live out his teachings with courage, even in what appeared to be the darkest of circumstances.

As my mind caught hold upon these thoughts, I could not help but think of Jesus standing calm and serene before the Sanhedrin. He did not allow their anger and hatred to penetrate his soul. I must not allow my own doubts to rob me of the light that I had experienced.

With a flash of understanding, the dreams of the night in Gethsemane came flooding into my mind. Jesus had overcome all the darkness that the world would know. He could give that strength to me. With these thoughts, the feeling of our embrace in the garden came rushing to my heart. It took my breath away. I began to weep uncontrollably.

My wife sat down on the bed next to me and held me close. She did not say anything, but she sat silently, holding me in an embrace that reminded me of that which I felt from the Savior. Her faith in Jesus had transformed her into a conduit of his love. I felt all fear and doubt depart as her love and tenderness filled my soul with love. I could feel that she not only believed in the teachings of Jesus as the Messiah, but she believed him too. She accepted fully his love for her and all of God's children. His love transformed her, and it was now reaching out to envelop me. I felt all doubt depart as I basked in the warmth of his love expressed through the embrace of my wife. In her embrace, we became united with the love of the Savior.

I realized in that moment that I did have much cause to worship and to celebrate. I had walked with the very Son of God and witnessed his love and mercy. I had been taught how to live and how to love. I felt as if I had been given the privilege of being on the top of a mountain, seeing life and living on a grander scale. I realized that while I was no longer on the mountaintop, I could live my life by the memory of what I had seen while I had been on the peak. This realization helped me to understand that every moment of life was not going to be filled with beautiful vistas, but all of life can be lived with the memory of the joy and beauty that one has witnessed. I wanted to now live my life by the memory of the joy I had experienced while living in the way that the Savior taught. He may have gone to heaven to be with his Father, but I could now work to make my own heaven on earth by living according to his teachings.

With this change of view and perspective on life, I joined my wife in honoring the Savior on this day of Sabbath, a day that God had provided in his goodness to remember his creation of this earth and his love and mercy in bringing our fathers out of the bondage of Egypt. I committed in my heart to also make the Sabbath a day for me to remember his Son and commit myself to live as he taught. I spent a good part of the day trying to write and remember all my experiences with Jesus as well as the lessons I had learned. This journal you are reading is a result of those efforts. It has served to help me put my experiences with Jesus into perspective and helped me to not only remember the light I have witnessed but to shine the light in my times of darkness as well.

Chapter 26

He Is Risen

The morning following the Sabbath was bright and clear. It was as if my new perspective about following the teachings of Jesus had breathed new life not only into me but also into the entire earth. Spring was now in its full splendor, and I felt the joy of the flowers and the plants as they awakened from their winter slumber. I had always enjoyed the time of Passover as a time that seemed to signal the passing over of death to life and the world becoming new again. This day seemed to dawn especially bright.

My wife was up and dressed as I came down from our bedroom into the kitchen. She informed me that she was joining several of the women in going to the tomb of Jesus to finish the anointing of his body with perfumes and oils. Christ had died so close to the time of preparation for the Sabbath that there had not been time to properly prepare his body before placing it in the tomb.

Before she departed, I held her in a lengthy embrace and thanked her for bringing the light back to my life when I had become shaken in my faith. It was still hard to believe that Jesus was gone, but I realized that we must go forward with our lives, strive to live what he taught, and help others to do the same. She kissed me gently on the cheek and thanked me for choosing to look to the light rather than the darkness of the moment. Then I saw her lip begin to quiver.

"I know that we must move forward," she said serenely, "but I feel like a part of my heart will always carry the ache of his absence."

"I understand," I replied. "I doubt that we will ever move completely beyond a portion of the emptiness that we feel, but I believe now that that is simply evidence of the depth of our love for him ... and the feeling of his love for us. As long as we remember him, we will forever have a space in our hearts for his love to fill."

My wife looked up at me in amazement. She marveled at the change that had come into me since the darkness of the previous day. I surprised myself by the clarity I now seemed to possess. He had told us that he would die. He also said that it was required so that he might provide for our salvation. I could still sense a feeling of longing in my heart, but I also felt the strength that had come in remembering the things he had taught.

"I am going with Cleopus to Emmaus today to purchase some fabric for the store," I said. "Will you return before I leave?"

"We should not be long," she replied. "Perhaps you could fix us some breakfast and we could eat together before you go?" She smiled and gave me a wink, knowing that I didn't ever make breakfast. I rolled my eyes and told her that I would give it my best effort. We embraced once more, and she departed to go with the other women.

I returned to our room to dress and clean up for the day. I could not help but wonder at the perspective that I had gained in one short day. Jesus was still gone, and many would surely persecute all who continued to follow his teachings. I felt certain that the Sanhedrin would work to quell any attempts to keep Jesus's teachings alive. Undoubtedly, life would be more difficult and challenging without the Savior among us, but somehow I still felt that by continuing to live his teachings, we would find joy amidst our trials. I was determined to never lose faith again. I realized that the choice about how I was going to live was now mine.

I was halfway through my preparations for breakfast when my wife came rushing into the room. Half out of breath from her hurried return, she gasped, "He is risen!"

I grasped her by the shoulders. "What? Who? What do you mean he is risen?"

"We went to the tomb to finish the anointing of Jesus's body and found Mary Magdalene on her way back from the tomb. She had gone early to the tomb and had found it empty. Two angels had told her that Jesus had risen and that she should go and tell the apostles. She ran and told Peter and John, who then went to the tomb. They saw the empty tomb, but they doubted that Jesus was risen. Mary told us that she had remained after Peter and John had departed and met a man she had thought to be the gardener. 'Then he spoke my name,' she almost whispered to us. She said that as he spoke, her eyes were opened and her heart was touched, and she saw that it was Jesus risen from the tomb."

My wife continued, "We all went to the tomb to see for ourselves, and two angels appeared to us, speaking words that penetrated my heart with a joy and hope that I had only known when I had touched his robe. 'He is risen. He is not here!'"

I looked at her in stunned amazement, unable to fully comprehend or believe what she was telling me. I searched her eyes, which filled with tears as she said, "That is not all." She sobbed. "The angels told us to go and testify to the apostles that Jesus is risen. We all departed quickly, running with the excitement of the news. Suddenly before our eyes, there he stood! Jesus is not dead but alive! He was radiating a light so bright that we could scarcely look upon him! We all fell at his feet and began to cry for joy and disbelief."

She looked deep into my eyes as she continued, "The others ran to tell the apostles, but I came straight to you. I wanted to share this moment with you." She must have seen the doubt in my eyes. She looked pleadingly into my eyes as she asked, "You do believe me, don't you?"

I hesitated. I wanted to believe her. I truly wanted to believe. I had no doubt that my wife believed that she had actually seen him, but my logical mind wondered if maybe her great love for Jesus and her faith to believe that he was not really dead had overcome her heart and mind.

"My love, I am sure that you have been blessed by the Lord to receive peace from the horror of what we witnessed. I would desire nothing more than for Jesus to be among us again. But it is as you said. As long as we live his teachings, he is alive in us."

"But I did see him!" she insisted. "You must believe me. Please allow yourself the faith to believe, and I am sure that you, too, will know for yourself that he is risen!"

I took her into my arms and whispered, "I will try. I will try." With all my soul, I wanted to believe her, but I was afraid to allow myself to open my heart again to the possibility that I would once again see the Savior. We stood embracing for several moments as I pondered the possibility. It seemed more than my mind could accept.

"I must be on my way," I said. "Cleopus is probably already waiting for me at the crossroads. I will return tomorrow toward evening if all goes well with the vendor."

She looked up into my eyes, pleading once again for me to believe.

"Please understand," I said softly. "I do desire to believe, but I am also afraid to allow myself to hope for something that may open me to the pain of losing Jesus once again."

"Remember," she whispered, "it is fear that causes us to drown in the seas of our own doubts."

Her words struck a chord of truth within my heart. I knew that I would have to overcome my fear if I was to find the faith to believe that Jesus was truly risen from the grave. I nodded and assured her that I would ponder these things as I journeyed. I kissed her goodbye and made my way to the crossroads to meet up with Cleopus.

Chapter 27

The Road to Understanding

As I had suspected, Cleopus was already waiting for me when I arrived. He greeted me warmly and asked what had kept me. I told him of the experience I had just had with my wife.

"She really believes that Jesus is risen from the tomb and that she saw him?" he inquired.

"Yes, she does," I replied. "But I saw him die on the cross. How could he yet be alive?" I said as we began our journey to Emmaus. "With all my heart, I would like to believe that he has overcome death itself, but how could that be? If he did have such power, why did he not step forward as the Messiah and free us all? Why leave us to continue to suffer at the hands of Roman injustices? Was this only to save himself and not us?"

As we discussed these confusing ideas, a stranger came and began walking alongside of us. We had not really noticed him at first, thinking that he was simply walking the same road that we traveled. He matched our pace for several steps and then asked, "What manner of communications are these that ye have one to another, as ye walk, and are sad?"

Cleopas responded, "Art thou only a stranger in Jerusalem, and hast not known the things which are come to pass there in these days?"[119]

The stranger inquired, "What things?"

"Concerning Jesus of Nazareth, which was a prophet mighty in deed and word before God and all the people," we explained. "And the chief priests and our rulers delivered him to be condemned to death and have crucified him."

"But we trusted that it had been he which should have redeemed Israel: and beside all this, today is the third day since these things were done. Yea, and certain women also of our company made us astonished, which were early at the sepulcher; and when they found not his body, they came, saying, that they had also seen a vision of angels, which said that he was alive. And certain of them which were with us went to the sepulcher, and found it even so as the women had said: but him they saw not."

Then he spoke unto us, saying, "O fools, and slow of heart to believe all that the prophets have spoken: Ought not Christ to have suffered these things, and to enter into his glory?"[120]

Then, beginning at Moses and all the prophets, he began to expound to us from the scriptures all things concerning Jesus.

As we walked and talked with this man, I marveled at his command of the scriptures. It was as if he was pouring light into my heart and mind. My heart burned within me as I felt the things he taught, every word testifying of Jesus. I looked closely at him and wondered why I had not seen him earlier among the disciples. As we drew nigh unto the village and the place where we were to stay, he acted as though he would continue farther on his journey.

I quickly entreated him, "Please, abide with us: for it is toward evening, and the day is far spent."[121] To my great joy, he agreed to remain with us and share our evening meal.

As we sat down to eat, our new friend took bread, blessed it, broke it, and gave some to each of us. As we ate the bread blessed by this stranger, all that Jesus had said and done while in the upper room seemed to come together in my heart and mind. In an instant my eyes were opened, and I knew him—Jesus! I gasped as my eyes began to swell with tears. I looked down to wipe my eyes, and suddenly, he disappeared from before us. Emotion overwhelmed me, and I began to sob.

I turned incredulously to Cleopus. He, too, was wiping tears from his eyes, marveling at what we had witnessed. We looked at each other in a state of disbelief. Then a confirming witness of peace came into my heart, and I knew!

"Did not our heart burn within us," I said to Cleopus, "while he talked with us by the way, and while he opened to us the scriptures?[122] Surely, we have been given a special witness and must share this with the apostles."

Chapter 28

Sharing and Receiving the Greater Witness

Forgetting our business, we immediately returned to Jerusalem. We heard word that the apostles had gathered at the home of one of the disciples, so we made our way to tell them the good news. The day was far spent and night had fallen when we finally arrived back in Jerusalem. We found ten of the apostles gathered together, talking about the events of the last few days and wondering particularly at the words of the women who had testified that Jesus had risen. I approached Peter, who stood and embraced me. After a brief welcome, Peter could tell that I was excited about something. I did not know how to say what was in my heart. "Friend," he said, "what is it? Is there something you want to tell us?"

"We have seen him," I said boldly. "We have seen the Lord."

We spent the next several minutes sharing with them what we had experienced, testifying that Jesus was indeed risen. While Peter nodded, seeming to acknowledge the truth of our words, others had doubts.

"I do not understand," said Matthew. "If this was the Lord, why did you not recognize him when you first met? You walked and talked with him for hours, yet you did not know him? How can it be that you knew him not?"

"Perhaps it was an angelic messenger rather than the Lord himself," offered James. "Certainly, an angel would be able to teach you the words of Jesus with such power that you might have been persuaded to think that it was the Lord?"

"It was the Lord!" I stated emphatically. "The Holy Spirit bore witness to our souls as he opened the scriptures to our understanding. We saw him bless and break the bread as he had done at other times, just as he did in the upper chamber of my in-laws' home. I know with all my soul that it was him. My wife told me that she had seen him, but I doubted her just as you now doubt me. But there is no more doubt in my mind. All darkness of doubt has been swept away by the light of the Spirit that has touched my mind and heart. I do not know why we did not recognize him in the beginning. Perhaps our sorrows so consumed our hearts that we could not see with our spiritual eyes what was before us. But no longer. I have felt the joy of the Lord's light and love and know that he is risen." I could see that the boldness of my witness caused them to wonder, but many still did not believe.[123]

Again, Peter approached me and put his hand upon my shoulder. "You have been one of the most faithful disciples since the beginning. The Spirit convinces me that you have spoken the truth. I do not doubt that you have seen the Lord. I do not know what we are to do now, but I am certain that the Lord's work is not over and that we will be a part of whatever is to come. Thank you for your witness."

"Thank you for believing me," I replied.

As we spoke, the room began to fill with a light that enveloped our hearts with a sense of holiness. Suddenly, Jesus himself stood in the midst of us, speaking softly the words, "Peace be unto you."[124]

I could see in the eyes of many that they were terrified and afraid, not knowing what they were seeing. Jesus inquired, "Why are ye troubled? and why do thoughts arise in your hearts? Behold my hands and my feet, that it is I myself: handle me, and see; for a spirit hath not flesh and bones, as ye see me have."[125]

Jesus extended his hands and invited each to come and see. We saw the prints of the nails where he had been fastened to the cross. As I saw the marks of the nails graven upon his hands, the words he had spoken to me on the road to Jerusalem came flooding back into my mind. "Even in the times when thou dost forget, yet will I not forget thee. I will engraven thee upon the palms of my hands that thou mayest know my love and become all that I have shown unto thee."

A flood of understanding and emotion washed over me. He had suffered all this because he knew it was the only way to make it possible for me to become what he had seen in me! Then my vision expanded to see that he had done this for all mankind, not just me! He saw infinite potential in every one of his brothers and sisters upon this earth. They were not mere mortals but all possible gods and goddesses, each with unlimited and divine potential. He had taken the load or weight of the glory of all of us upon him, atoning for our sins and making right every injustice that would come in our lives.

My dreams of Gethsemane came clearly into my mind. I realized now that it had not been a dream. He had suffered as I had seen. He had taken all our burdens upon him, and now in a covenantal token of remembering each of us, he had allowed himself to be crucified, engraving forever upon himself the memory of the price that he paid to save and redeem every child of his Father in heaven. Truly, the worth of each soul was great in the sight of God and Jesus, his only begotten Son!

As I became overwhelmed at all the light flooding into my heart and mind, some of the apostles were still struggling to accept that this was truly Jesus resurrected from the tomb. Even with this sure witness, some felt as if this was a thing too good to be true, and they were blinded to the fact that this was truly Jesus in the flesh. While they yet believed not for joy, and wondered, he said unto them, "Have ye here any meat?"[126] They quickly brought him a piece of a broiled fish and some honeycomb. He took it and ate it so that they could see that he was truly flesh and bone and not simply a spirit or apparition.

For a brief moment, Jesus paused and looked around the room at each of us. As Jesus's gaze fell upon me, my heart felt the peace and calm that had always accompanied his presence. He smiled and looked into my eyes. Once again, I felt his love and vision for who I was to become, now made fully possible because of his offering. I felt renewed and whole as never before in my life.

Jesus began to explain how all that had transpired had come together as it had been prophesied. "These are the words which I spoke unto you, while I was yet with you, that all things must be fulfilled, which were written in the law of Moses, and in the prophets, and in the psalms, concerning me."[127]

Then as he had done with me and Cleopus on the road to Emmaus, he taught us and opened our hearts so that we might understand the scriptures, saying, "Thus it is written, and thus it behooved Christ to suffer, and to rise from the dead the third day; that repentance and remission of sins should be preached in his name among all nations, beginning at Jerusalem."[128]

At this saying, Jesus turned to Peter and explained that we were to go to all nations throughout the world to be his witnesses in all these things. He blessed and instructed us, "Ye are witnesses of these things. Behold, I send the promise of my Father upon you: but tarry ye in the city of Jerusalem, until ye be endowed with power from on high."[129]

Following these words, the light began to gather around Jesus until he became so luminescent that I could not see him for the brightness thereof. In an instant the light departed from the room, and Jesus was gone. Our time with him was brief, but it left a lasting impression upon every fiber of my soul.

No one spoke. All were overwhelmed at what had taken place. The room remained silent for several moments. Peter finally broke the silence. "Brethren," he said, "we have all been blessed this day so that we might be witnesses of his resurrection. Let us go to our homes, ponder on these things, and thank God for his divine Son and the glory of what we have witnessed."

We bid one another farewell and departed for the evening. As we left the room, Peter took my hand and thanked me for my witness. I assured him that I would be forever grateful to have been a part of such a sacred evening.

Though I had walked all day, I felt energy growing with every step toward home. I could not wait to share with my wife the events that had transpired. I was certain that she would be asleep, but I knew that I could not wait until the morning to share the news of what I had experienced.

Quietly ascending the stairs and approaching the door to our room, I heard her softly speaking to someone. I paused at the door to listen. She was praying … for me! She was asking the Lord to share with me the witness of what she knew—that Jesus was alive and was risen from the tomb. I could hardly hold back the tears as I listened to her pray unto the Father on my behalf.

She paused in her pleadings, and I slowly entered the room. I quietly went over and knelt next to her by the bed, placing my arm around her. A bit surprised, she looked at me. Only a small lamp burned in the corner, but I could see that her eyes were wet with tears. She tenderly reached up to touch my face and then gently kissed my cheek. Still somewhat confused, she asked, "What are you doing here? I thought you were spending the night in Emmaus."

I shook my head. "I had intended to be there overnight, but something wonderful has happened that I had to share with you."

I told her of our walk with Jesus along the road to Emmaus and about not recognizing who he was until he blessed and broke the bread. Joy and gratitude swept over her face. She threw her arms about my neck and began to kiss me repeatedly. She had worried that I would allow my doubts to keep me from knowing and seeing what she had witnessed. "The Lord is gracious and has answered my prayers!" she whispered.

"That is not all," I replied. "Cleopus and I returned immediately to tell the apostles what we had seen. They were reluctant to believe us just as I had been hesitant when you shared your experience with me." At this, I squeezed her hand to let her know of my love and regret that I had not been more trusting of her testimony.

She smiled and returned my squeeze.

I continued, "After I had shared with them the certainty of our experience, the room began to fill with light. To my amazement, Jesus appeared. Some of the men were frightened and had a difficult time believing that it was the Lord, so he demonstrated that he was flesh and bones by having us touch him. He also ate some fish and honeycomb. But it was not until Jesus taught from the scriptures that they were able to finally comprehend that he was resurrected and standing before them in a physical body."

"You touched him?" she asked.

"As I am touching you now," I responded. "It was as if he had never died but had simply been away on a journey. He is risen just as you had said. I now know as you know, and we are to be witnesses to all of the world that he lives."

Chapter 29

Believing Is Seeing

We sat in silence for a few moments. My mind began to reflect upon my experience on the way to Emmaus. I turned to my wife, asking quietly, "Why do you think that I did not recognize him when I first met him on the road to Emmaus."

She became thoughtful for a few moments before answering. "You said that when he gave you of the bread, your eyes were opened and that your heart had burned within you while he taught you the scriptures. Perhaps we must first have faith and believe his words before we are able to see miracles."

She continued, "The truth is often given to us a little at a time until we are prepared and willing to accept it in our hearts. It seems that the bread and wine were reminders to your heart of what Jesus had taught about being the Bread of Life. Simple symbols often have hidden power to open our eyes and turn our hearts to God."

Then almost as an afterthought, she added, "I wonder if all the ordinances that our people have been observing for these thousands of years were all designed to show us the true nature of Jesus, but we as a people have been too focused on the symbols instead of what they symbolized?"

Her words sent light blazing with truth into every corner of my mind. "That is why he continually opened the scriptures," I cried.

"He wanted us to believe what he said so that we could see him for who he truly is! Seeing is not believing, but believing is seeing!"

It all seemed so clear to me now. As Jews, we had trusted in the law and the scriptures as the way for us to return to God, but all scripture was written to bear record of him. He is the only way for us to return to God! But we had missed the mark and the meaning of the Messiah.

Suddenly, many of the ancient writings took on new meaning. My mind raced back to the beginning of the scriptures, allowing me to see Jesus in many things that I had not recognized before. The animal sacrificed to provide a coat of skins to cover Adam and Eve after they had tried to cover their nakedness with fig leaves became a symbol of the covering the Messiah would provide for us through his atoning sacrifice.

Abraham and his willingness to sacrifice Isaac was the story of God's willingness to sacrifice his Son for all of us. Isaac had been required to carry the wood just as Jesus had had to carry his cross. And while Isaac had been spared, there was no ram in the thicket this time to provide a substitute sacrifice for Jesus.

I thought about Joseph, who had been betrayed by his brothers, yet he became the very person who would provide a way of salvation for all Israel. And there was Moses, who had escaped the edict of death upon the children. This now seemed but a type and shadow of the infant Jesus who was spared from the edict of Herod. Moses had delivered Israel from Egypt just as we are delivered from our sins by Jesus, the true deliverer.

Of course, there was the Passover pointing to Jesus, but even more, the entire exodus from Egypt to the Promised Land became in my mind a journey that testified to me of our need for Jesus along our journey back to God. The parting of the Red Sea, the pillar of fire and cloud of smoke guiding them in their journey, the manna in the desert, the water from the rock—these all testified of Jesus as the way back to God.

I now understood why it was Joshua—the Hebrew name for Jesus—who led Israel into the Promised Land instead of Moses.

This was to show us that it was not the law of Moses but Jesus, the true Messiah, that would take all mankind into God's presence.

So many examples flooded into my mind that my thoughts became a whirlwind of witnesses to Jesus and his role as the Savior—Abigail's offering to David, the temptation and fall of the kings of Israel, the cry of the psalmist about being forsaken, the story of Jonah. All of these and hundreds of others pointed unmistakably to Jesus!

The words of Jesus to the Pharisees resonated with truth. "Search these scriptures; for in them ye think ye have eternal life: and they are they which testify of me."[130] I could not help but now see through the power of the Spirit that all things from the beginning had been given to testify of Jesus and his role to bring all of us to salvation.

Amid all the scriptures pressing themselves into my mind in just those few short moments, the story of Jonah continually returned to my thoughts. I hurriedly retrieved the scriptures that were on the table near our bed. I rifled through the scroll to find the passages of Jonah, excitedly sharing with my wife what I was witnessing. She joined in my excitement to have the scriptures opened to our understanding by the Spirit.

As we reviewed the story together, I realized that Jonah had been called to preach to a wicked nation just as Jesus had been sent to the unbelieving Jews. I pointed out to my wife the parallel between Jonah sleeping on the boat and the night that we had been on the Sea of Galilee and had been caught in a storm that we all feared would cast us into the sea. The Master had calmed the storm just as Jonah being cast over the side had calmed the seas. I had not realized at the time that Jesus would give his life to calm the storms in my life if I would but put my trust in him and obey his commands.

When we read of the weeds about Jonah's head, I could not help but think of the crown of thorns that had been placed on the head of the Savior. In the darkness of his anguish, Jonah had called out to God just as I had heard Jesus call unto his Father about being forsaken. Jonah's three days in the belly of the fish was a powerful parallel to the three days the Savior had spent in the tomb. Yet just as Jonah came forth, Christ also arose from death to go forth and preach again.

As all these truths from the story of Jonah sunk deep into my heart, I could not help but think that this was what the Savior meant when he told the Pharisees, "This is an evil generation: ye seek a sign; and there shall no sign be given, but the sign of Jonah the prophet."[131] Certainly, the sign of Jonah was enough to show any man that Jesus was sent to save all mankind by giving his life for us. Truly, the story of Jonah was the symbol of his death and resurrection in order to save us all.

My wife and I marveled at how clearly the scriptures testified of all that Jesus would do, and yet we had not seen. It was a fitting parallel to my experience in not recognizing the Savior on the road to Emmaus. It was not until he revealed himself to me—through the scriptures he had taught and the bread and wine he had blessed for me—that I was finally able to see him as the resurrected Lord. Truly reading the scriptures and the participating in the ordinances would never again be things that I did without seeing and acknowledging Jesus.

I invited my wife to pray as we knelt by our bed before retiring for the evening. She expressed the joy we felt in a way that left me forever grateful that we were companions. She was truly an angel sent to help me see, feel, and know God's love. Together we had come to believe and finally see the ultimate manifestation of that love. Truly, God so loved all of us that he gave his only begotten Son so that whosoever believeth in him should not perish but have everlasting life.[132]

Chapter 30

Living and Becoming

The news that Jesus's body was not in the tomb brought a myriad of mixed responses over the next several days and weeks. The Pharisees proclaimed that his body had been stolen by his disciples to give the appearance that he was resurrected. They tried to stop any talk of Jesus being the true Messiah who had given his life for us and then taken it up again. Some people sided with the Sanhedrin, but more and more of the people believed in the words of the witnesses. Those who spoke openly about having seen Jesus received both persecution and praise.

I returned to my work in the shop of my father-in-law, but I looked for every opportunity to share what I had witnessed. A few days after Jesus's resurrection, Luke came in to visit with me. He had heard the news and had moved to Jerusalem with his family so that he might more fully follow Jesus. I shared with him my experiences on the road to Emmaus and seeing Jesus among the apostles. He absorbed all that I said with the feverish excitement of a child during the days of the great feast. He scribbled as fast as he could so as to capture every detail. Our friendship grew stronger and stronger as he returned again and again to write about my experiences in my journeys with Jesus.

Peter asked my wife's parents if the apostles could use the upper room in their home to meet with all the disciples each week. They were honored and overjoyed to provide a place for these gatherings. We began to meet with the apostles on the first day of each week, honoring the day on which Jesus had risen from the tomb. The apostles testified that Jesus had appeared again to them just eight days after his resurrection. Thomas shared how he had doubted the previous witnesses but now had come to know for himself that Jesus lived.

At each of our weekly meetings, we would partake of bread and wine as a token to remember Jesus. Peter told us that the Savior had instituted this "sacrament" as he called it while they had shared the Passover with him in this very room. He told us that it was to take the place of the Passover, pointing us to the fact that the Lamb of God had been slain for all. He taught us that the law of Moses had been fulfilled in Jesus's teachings and sacrificial offering for us.

These meetings were a time when Peter and the apostles taught us many doctrines they said Jesus had been teaching them during various visits in the days that followed the resurrection. One doctrine Peter shared was that Jesus had visited the spirits in the spirit world while his body laid in the tomb and that the Lord had established an organization among them so that the spirits in prison might be taught and receive the good news of Jesus and his atonement, which they had not received during their time on earth. By beginning this work, Peter told us that it would now be possible for all mankind who had ever lived on the earth to know of Jesus.[133]

My heart leaped within me at such doctrine. I thought about my family and my first wife, who had died without ever having a chance to hear and know the truths Jesus taught. I had always wondered how God could be a loving and caring Father to all his children if many had come to this earth in a time and place when they would not be able to hear the good news of the Savior. This doctrine was as sweet honey to my soul, and I felt the Spirit bear witness to my heart of God's love and concern for all his children. In my mind's eye, I could see my father and mother meeting Jesus on the other side along with my first wife and my siblings, who had all passed to the other side. My heart overflowed with the joy that

I felt as the Spirit confirmed the truth of this marvelous doctrine coming from the lips of God's chosen servants.

My wife and I were thrilled to meet in our home with all the disciples each week. We developed a love and communion with all who believed on Jesus. Luke and his family joined with us in worshipping the Lord, remembering him through the sacrament, and speaking of his doctrine to love all men.

One day as we entered the upper room to meet as disciples, we were surprised to find that Peter and several others of the apostles were not present. I asked Matthew why they were not with us. He replied that Peter along with James, John, Thomas, and Nathanael had all gone back to Galilee, where they intended to return to their trade as fishermen.

I could not believe what I was hearing. My wife and I exchanged puzzled looks. My wife asked Matthew incredulously, "What are we to do? Are we to hold the meeting without them? How are we to be taught if we have no prophet to instruct us?"

Matthew shrugged his shoulders. "You have asked the questions that are in the heart of all of us, dear sister. We are not certain what we are to do now. Those of us whom Jesus ordained to be apostles can continue to teach, but Jesus bestowed upon Peter, James, and John the keys of the presidency when he took them up to the Mount Heron. There he was transfigured before them, and received keys from Moses, Elias, and Elijah.[134] Without those keys, we are not fully authorized to lead or organize the disciples. We are seeing new converts added to our numbers each day, but we are uncertain how we are to proceed."

As the meeting ended, we were a bit troubled and uncertain about what was ahead for us as disciples of Jesus. We had our testimonies and our faith to carry us forward, but we felt a longing to be united with others who wanted to follow the teachings of the Master. Our weekly worship had become a treasured way for us to remember Jesus and become more committed to live as he taught. We did not want this to come to an end, but we also wanted to follow the prophetic keys Jesus himself had given.[135]

The thought crossed my mind that perhaps I should return to Galilee and restart my business there where I could be closer to Peter and the other apostles. When I shared the idea with my wife, she was reluctant.

"If we leave my parents," she began slowly, "what will happen to them and their ability to remain true to the Savior? Certainly, none of their friends in the Sanhedrin will be sympathetic or understanding of their beliefs. I fear that they may find it difficult to remain true if we are not here."

I realized quickly that she was right and that we were to stay in Jerusalem and continue to help her parents and others in the area to remain faithful, hoping that word would soon come from Peter and the others of what we were to do.

To our great joy, it was only a few days before Peter returned to Jerusalem with the other apostles. They shared in one of our meetings how they had been fishing on the Sea of Galilee when the Savior had appeared to them. Peter told how the Savior had asked him three times if he loved him, and then Jesus made the powerful point that if Peter truly loved him, he would feed his sheep.

Peter spoke with boldness. "After hearing Jesus's words to me, I realized that I needed to give up my former life and return to Jerusalem to lead his disciples. After our arrival, we gathered the apostles together to decide how we were going to fulfill Jesus's words to feed his sheep. As we met together, the Lord came unto us and instructed us that we are not to leave Jerusalem until we have received the Spirit that he promised us while meeting during the Passover. He told us that not only were we baptized by water but that we would also be baptized with fire by the Holy Ghost."[136]

Peter continued, "Jesus spake unto us, saying, 'Ye shall receive power, and after that the Holy Ghost is come upon you: and ye shall be witnesses unto me both in Jerusalem, and in all Judaea, and in Samaria, and unto the uttermost parts of the earth.'[137] After leaving us with this great commission to go to all the world, Jesus was then taken up into heaven in a cloud. As we stood wondering and amazed, two angels stood by us and witnessed to us that Jesus would come again to the earth in the clouds of heaven."

This news from Peter caused joy and happiness to fill every corner of my soul. Jesus had not left us alone, but he had simply opened the door for all of us to be able to return to our Father in heaven. Now he had established his gospel through apostles and prophets to lead and guide us and to help us remember and unite as believers to follow his teachings. There were over one hundred of us gathered together in the upper room of my parents' home. We sang praises, took of the bread and wine in remembrance of Jesus, and spoke together of his eternal love and sacrifice for us.

My wife reached over and grasped my hand. I could not imagine a more joyful moment as we sang the song of redeeming love from the words of the psalmist. "The Lord is my Shepherd, I shall not want. He maketh me to lie down in green pastures: he leadeth me beside the still waters. He restoreth my soul: he leadeth me in the paths of righteousness for his name's sake. Yea, though I walk through the valley of the shadow of death, I will fear no evil: for thou art with me; thy rod and thy staff they comfort me. Thou preparest a table before me in the presence of mine enemies: thou anointest my head with oil; my cup runneth over. Surely goodness and mercy shall follow me all the days of my life: and I will dwell in the house of the Lord forever."[138]

As the singing ended, the happiness of this moment filled my heart. Peter again stood before our group of worshippers. He told us that one of the first orders of business in our newly organized church was to ordain a new apostle to fill the place of Judas, who had betrayed Jesus and taken his life. He said that the new apostle would be chosen from among those who had been with Jesus from the beginning and would now stand as a witness of Jesus as the Messiah of the Jews and Savior for all the world.

My head quickly dropped in disbelief as my name was mentioned among those who had been appointed as possible apostles of the Lord. I was overwhelmed at the thought of this sacred calling. My wife slipped her arm through mine, squeezed, and pressed her cheek against my arm.

To stand as a witness to the world that Jesus is the Savior! That he lives! Jesus, whom I had loved from the time he was but a babe in Bethlehem. Jesus who had taught me, loved me, and cared for me. I was amazed at the love that Jesus had offered me. As I thought on all that had transpired, I was confused at his grace that so fully he had made available to me through my life, even though I had not always been valiant, even though I had sinned many times. I then thought of how he had suffered and bled for me in Gethsemane and died for me on the cross at Calvary. Tears swelled up in my eyes.

Thinking back on all that had taken place, I could not help but think how wonderful it had all been. Suddenly, a smile came across my face. All these had been offered to me without a calling or position to make it so! I had been his disciple. That was all that mattered! I had chosen to love him, to follow him, and to reach out to serve him and my fellow man.

In those few moments, I thought back to when I had first met my wife. She had come, unknown to all of us, and had simply touched his hem. No fanfare, no calling, just a longing for the healing touch of the Master. In contrast to her unseen seeking, there was all of us—pushing and jostling to be near to Jesus—hoping for some special place, station, or recognition. It all seemed a bit foolish now.

My smile broadened as I took hold of my wife's arm, which was clinging to mine. I looked into her eyes as the lots were cast to choose the new apostle. The name that was chosen was not important. I realized that the choosing was his, not mine. I would be a witness for him and serve him all my life regardless of the position or calling I would hold.

As these thoughts entered my heart, I felt the Spirit whisper to my soul. I could see in my mind's eye the vision of myself each time that I had looked into the eyes of Jesus. As in the day when I first kissed him on the head as an infant, the desire to just be good filled every fiber of my soul. I finally felt his peace and the joy of becoming the man Jesus had made it possible for me to be—perhaps unknown to the world, but known to him. I had now become his true disciple.

Endnotes

1 Luke 2:10–12
2 Luke 2:14 Vulgate version
3 Luke 2:15
4 Words taken from a variety of modern Christmas songs, including "O Holy Night," "Silent Night," "Handel's Messiah," "Go Tell It on the Mountains," "What Child Is This?"
5 Luke 2:49
6 John 4:29
7 John 4:26
8 John 6:38
9 Matthew 16:24
10 Luke 5:5–6
11 Luke 5:20
12 Luke 5:21
13 Luke 5:22–24
14 Matthew 9:13
15 Matthew 9:16–17
16 Luke 8:22
17 Matthew 8:24–26; Mark 4:38–41; Luke 8:23–25. The wording here is derived by blending the accounts of this event from all three synoptic writers.
18 Luke 8:43–45
19 Luke 8:46
20 Luke 8:48
21 Matthew 25:21, 23
22 Matthew 25:40
23 Luke 7:48, 50
24 Matthew 14:26–29
25 Matthew 14:30–31
26 John 6:26–27
27 John 6:32–33

28 John 6:34
29 John 6:35
30 John 6:48–51
31 John 6:53–56
32 John 6:60–63
33 John 6:67–69
34 Matthew 16:13–14
35 Matthew 16:15
36 Matthew 16:16–19
37 Matthew 16:21–23
38 Luke 9:23–26
39 Luke 9:55–56
40 Luke 10:25–29
41 Luke 10:30–37
42 John 7:37–38
43 John 8:7
44 John 8:10–11
45 Matthew 10:39
46 John 8:12
47 John 8:13–19
48 John 8:28–29
49 John 8:31–32
50 John 8:33
51 John 8:34–36
52 John 8:39–45
53 John 8:48–59
54 Mark 9:31–32
55 John 9:8-11
56 See Isaiah 58:6–8, 13–14
57 John 9:35–39
58 John 9:40–41
59 See Isaiah 50:11
60 See John 10:1–5
61 See John 10:7–18
62 John 10:19–21
63 John 10:24–30
64 See John 10:31–38
65 Luke 18:19
66 Luke 18:18–22
67 Luke 18:24
68 Mark 10:24

69 These phrases are a combination of those given by Matthew and Luke. See Matthew 21:9 and Luke 19:38.
70 Luke 2:14 Vulgate version
71 Luke 19:39–40
72 Luke 19:46
73 Matthew 21:16
74 See Matthew 22:16-21
75 See Matthew 23:13-28
76 Proverbs 3:11–12
77 See 1 Samuel 16:7
78 See Luke 22:8-13
79 Matthew 26:22
80 John 13:27
81 John 13:6–9
82 John 13:12–16
83 John 14:6
84 John 14:27
85 These words are combined from Matthew 26:26–29 and Luke 22:19–20.
86 John 15:5–8
87 John 15:13
88 John 17:20–24
89 Mark 14:36
90 Isaiah 53:10
91 Matthew 26:42
92 See Luke 22:44 and Hebrews 12:4.
93 John 14:27
94 Luke 22:64
95 Luke 22:67–70
96 Mark 14:63-64
97 Luke 23:2
98 Luke 23:3
99 Luke 23:4
100 See Luke 23:5–7
101 See Luke 23:14–20
102 John 19:5
103 Isaiah 53:2–4
104 Luke 23:22
105 John 19:12
106 John 19:15
107 Matthew 27:24
108 Matthew 27:25

109 Luke 23:28–30
110 Luke 23:34
111 Matthew 5:44
112 Luke 23:39
113 Luke 23:40–43
114 John 17:24
115 John 19:26–27
116 Matthew 27:46
117 See John 16:32
118 These words are a combination of Luke 23:46 and John 19:30.
119 See Luke 24:15–18
120 See Luke 24:19–26
121 Luke 24:29
122 Luke 24:32
123 See Mark 16:12–13
124 Luke 24:36
125 Luke 24:38–39
126 Luke 24:41–43
127 Luke 24:44
128 Luke 24:46–47
129 Luke 24:48–49
130 John 5:39
131 Luke 11:29
132 John 3:16
133 See 1 Peter 3:18–20 and 1 Peter 4:6.
134 See Matthew 17:1–8.
135 See Matthew 16:15–19.
136 Acts 1:5
137 Acts 1:8
138 Psalm 23